QUEEN OF THE UNDERWORLD

TARTARUS

BOOK ONE

FoxTales Press

DANI HOOTS

Tartarus
Queen of the Underworld, #1
© 2021 FoxTales Press
Proofreading by Victory Editing
Cover Design Copyright © 2021 by Biserka
Designs
All rights reserved.

ISBN for paperback: 978-1-942023-87-6

ISBN for hardcover: 978-1-942023-88-3

CHAPTER ONE

Chrys

"Please! Please don't send me to hell! I beg you! If I had known there was an afterlife, I would have been better! Give me a second chance!" The man before me groveled on his knees.

This seemed familiar to me, perhaps because so many had begged in such a way throughout the centuries. I glanced over to the three stooges—Minos, Rhadamanthys, and Aiakos—who were all scrambling to write down notes. Apparently I judged faster than my father Hades had. It made sense. My heart was no longer in it—not since my father was wrongfully sent to Tartarus.

"To Tartarus. Cerberus!" I shouted for the puppy to come get his next victim.

Cerberus was definitely not a puppy, but I had grown up with him, and in my eyes he was just a cute, innocent animal. Cerberus came galloping into the room like a large, uncoordinated elephant, and he grabbed the man by the back of his suit jacket and dragged him to be flung into Tartarus. The man screamed the entire way.

I stood up and stretched. It had definitely been a long day, and I was ready to call it. The more years that had passed, the more humans it seemed needed to be judged. Were there really that many more people in the world, or was it just that many more were on the line between good and evil?

It didn't matter to me, however, as the underworld never ran out of room. It was cool but also a little unnerving.

"How many are left?" I asked the three stooges.

Minos peered up at me. "Uh, three more, goddess

Chrysanthemum."

I sighed. "How many times do I have to tell you? Just call me Chrys."

He nodded. "Right, sorry."

He was never going to get it. They rarely talked to me when Hades was around, and now that he was gone, they'd begun to acknowledge me with my full title. I didn't care for it as I didn't feel like this was the place where I belonged. It should be my father judging souls and sitting on the throne of the underworld, but it wasn't.

"Fine, send them in."

After the final three were judged, I quickly got out of the throne room and headed toward the balcony that overlooked the underworld.

This used to be my favorite place to look out and see my father's world, but now it was a place that only stabbed my heart and kept me moving toward the goal I wanted to achieve. The sky, which was made up of Oceanus, sparkled like lapis lazuli. In the center of the underworld was a waterfall of souls as they descended into Tartarus. Countless souls screamed as they fell into the pit of despair—where the Titans were chained for the rest of time.

Where my father was.

I wanted to cry, but the tears had run out months ago. Two years had passed now, and I wasn't any closer to achieving my goal. What was I supposed to do? How would I get my father back?

After the fight and everything had happened, I'd begged Hermes to try to fish him out like he had done for Huntley and me, but too much time had passed. When Huntley was sent to Tartarus, only a minute or so had gone by, and Hermes was at the ready. When my father was sent to Tartarus, a few hours had passed, not to mention that Kronos, my grandfather whom the Olympian gods had defeated and chained down there, would use all his power to pull any god down as fast as he could so that they could endure the same pain as he had.

I felt one tear escape and roll down my cheek. So I could still cry. That was a surprise. I wiped it away and closed my eyes. If I focused hard enough, I could almost hear Kronos's voice taunting me—telling me what eternal torment was like. I didn't want to hear it, but I couldn't help it. It was the only connection I had with my father even if it was gut-wrenching.

When I'd tried to find a way out of my marriage to Zeus, I had fallen into Tartarus. It was as if something had grabbed me and pulled me down. For a brief moment, I learned what eternal torment was actually like. I could hear a voice, and I still wasn't quite sure who or what it was.

I opened my eyes. It didn't seem I was going to get any information out of Kronos today. I took a deep breath and leaned forward against the rail.

This was all Zeus's fault. If he hadn't tried to kill me, then marry me, we wouldn't be in this mess. He didn't like my power, and because of it, he kept attacking me. Then my father had gotten in the middle and was banished from the world and stuck in Tartarus. I think Kronos did the same to Zeus and to Poseidon, and they were all down there now, enduring the wrath of their own father.

No, I couldn't just blame Zeus. This was also my fault. If I hadn't left the safety of the underworld—if I hadn't listened to AJ and gone to the mortal realm, this wouldn't have happened. If there was anyone to blame, it was me for not listening to my father. And AJ since he was the one who had informed his father Poseidon about my existence. I could blame him as well.

So much time had passed, and yet it felt like yesterday. I bit my lip, wondering if I should visit my mother anytime soon. She hadn't come back to the underworld since Father was sent to Tartarus as she no longer had a reason to come. I didn't feel that she didn't love me—she tried everything she could to save me from Zeus and then Prometheus and Apollo—but I was a little hurt that I hadn't heard a word from her since the funeral. Perhaps she was trying to give me space, but did I want space? No, I wanted my mother to comfort me. She had never understood that throughout the years.

It was getting late, and I knew Huntley was preparing dinner, and by preparing, I meant he was helping the chef pick out what to serve. Although Huntley was getting better at cooking, he wasn't nearly as good as the chef I had hired. Huntley was good at knowing what I wanted to eat at any given moment. It was as if he could read my mind.

Being officially husband and wife was rather strange. We had fought for our love and against Zeus for that entire year, and to find out that we had already been married was shocking to say the least. For the past two years, we had become closer, and Huntley was the first human prince of the underworld. He thought the title was cool, but I had a feeling it was a lot for him to handle. Not many humans became the spouses of gods and survived, although since we were in the underworld, it was a bit easier. He was already dead and could be there without any problems. I didn't have to worry about him dying—that is, as long as he wasn't sent to Tartarus.

Taking a deep breath, I headed toward the dining hall. I glanced down to find I was still wearing my queen-like dark dress. With a wave of my hand, I transformed my dress into some jeans and a band T-shirt that had the album cover for Die Kreatur's *Panoptikum*. It was a new album that I enjoyed a lot with Huntley, and he was able to snag it the last time he went up to visit Pothos and Mel. My long brown hair was no longer up in a cute bun but curly and down. I preferred it down, but it got in my way while judging.

Opening the doors to the dining hall, I found that dinner was cottage pie. The heavenly aroma of ground beef, thyme, and oregano came wafting to me. My stomach growled, and I was excited to eat, bringing my depressive state to a halt, at least for the time being. Huntley hurried to me, his shaggy brown hair clipped back and out of his face.

Huntley hugged me. "Did you have a good day?"

I nodded. "Yeah, same as usual."

"Well, that's good. I had the cook make some cottage pie and for drinks, Guinness of course."

I laughed. "Of course."

He grinned as he pulled my seat back for me. "I even got to help with the gravy. I added some Guinness in it to bring out the flavors. I hope you enjoy. And dessert is going to be even better!"

I raised an eyebrow as I took a seat. "Oh, and what is dessert going to be?"

"That's a secret." He also sat down. "Now let's dig in!"

I took a bite of the cottage pie. It was still steaming, and I burned my tongue a little, but it healed right away. One good thing about being a goddess was that I didn't have to wait for my food to cool. I couldn't imagine that burning sensation staying and it feeling off for a few days like Huntley told me about. That would suck.

"This is wonderful, Huntley! I'm so glad you found a fun hobby you love."

"Thank you. You know, you can always take a little time to find yourself a hobby. Seems like lately you just roam around, lost in thought."

I wasn't sure how to reply to that. Sure, I had been roaming around mindlessly, or at least that was what it looked like to others. Truth be told, I had been searching through all my father's things, looking for a way to open the gates to Tartarus. So far, I hadn't found anything.

"Besides zoning out and listening to music? I don't know, Huntley, that sort of is my favorite thing to do."

He laughed. "Yeah, that is fun."

"And I have a little less time than you in that regard. Just having some time to zone out is nice."

He didn't say anything but frowned. I felt a little bad, as I had suggested he didn't have an actual job down here, but that was true. He was human and didn't have powers. That didn't mean I loved him any less, not to mention his cooking skills were getting quite good.

We finished up our meal, and Huntley went into the kitchen to grab the dessert. When he came back, I found that he had made some crème brûlée. My eyes widened.

"You are the best!"

He grinned from ear to ear. "And don't you forget it!"

CHAPTER TWO

Huntley

It has been two years since Hades had, in a sense, died, and Chrys still wasn't back to her old self.

Granted, I never expected her to go back to normal, as losing a parent changed a person. One would always mourn, but there was something more with Chrys— something she wasn't telling me. Part of me wondered if she was trying to find a way to open Tartarus. I couldn't believe she would do that even if it was for her own father.

I had to admit, Hades's castle was rather quiet without him, especially since there were no more fights between him and Persephone. Chrys and I didn't argue, although we hadn't been a couple for as long as they had been. Even then, I doubted we would fight as we didn't have anyone on the outside trying to break us up. Persephone had everyone thinking Hades was a horrible person, and that pressure could build up. Also, Chrys wouldn't sleep with any other men. That was just a fact.

I got up out of bed and stretched. Chrys had already gotten up and gone to work. She was drowning herself in work to push back thoughts about her father, although I had a feeling it was doing the opposite. Everything down here would remind her of her father, not to mention she was acting more and more like him every day. At least she didn't threaten me like her father used to.

Smiling a little, I wondered what he would have said to me after everything was through and Chrys and I were officially married. He was going to chew me out. I just knew it. I wish he'd get the chance, as I'd rather have him hate me forever for taking his daughter than this.

But there was no use in wishing such things. No one escaped Tartarus.

Well, that wasn't true. I did, with Hermes's help. But that was different. He was able to because I was human and I hadn't fallen that deep. And my father wasn't down there waiting to take his revenge out on me. Well, maybe. If my father was dead, he would more than likely be in Tartarus.

I changed into some old clothes that I didn't mind getting dirty and headed toward the kitchen. The chef, Luc Madoc, had been a world-renowned chef from Wales. He was even on a few different baking and cooking shows before he passed on. Chrys hired him shortly after she'd became queen, and since then I have been learning from him. I had no idea what he had in store for me today, but I knew it would be fun.

Even after two years, I was nowhere as good as him, which made sense. He had been cooking for over forty years. Perhaps I would get as good as him and I would feel as if I had a place in the castle. I was prince of the underworld, or at least that was what many of the people who worked here called me. I didn't like the title as I did not feel like a prince. I just felt like some human who'd gotten caught up in the middle of some mythological tale. I wasn't a hero. I was just trying to save the girl I liked.

I arrived in the kitchen to find Luc gathering some items from the fridge and pantry. He noticed me walk in and clapped his hands together.

"Do I have a surprise for you!"

That was never good. I was glad I'd worn some old clothes because whenever he said he had a surprise, I got food all over myself. "And what's that?"

"Today we are going to make some ice cream!"

That sounded easy enough. I grabbed an apron, even though I knew it didn't matter what I wore over my clothes; they still got messy.

"Great. Where do I start?"

Ice cream should not be that hard to make. One had to add milk and then eggs with sugar, and it had to be mixed at just the right temperature and then the gelatin, and again, everything had to be at the exact temperature, and then after all that, we had to wait.

I don't know if people knew this about me, but I didn't like waiting. I was a bit impatient at times.

"You need to learn to be calm, Huntley. Otherwise, you will not be a great chef," Luc commented as he watched me move back and forth. His red hair was still styled like it had been that morning, unlike my hair, which I had run my hand through a million times.

"You sound like everyone else," I said as I stopped and rubbed my face.

"Regular life is different. As long as you aren't hurting anyone, impatience isn't a bad virtue to have. But when it comes to cooking, it could be the difference between the best dish in the world—or underworld— and the worst."

He had a point there. I had learned that the first time we'd made a cake. Let's just say I wasn't allowed to bake for a while.

Luc waved his hand. "Besides, we have already begun the broth for tonight's dish, and the eggs are in the fridge, soaking in soy sauce. Honestly, you could head out and get other things done. You don't have to wait here the entire four hours or so."

He was right. I didn't need to, but I didn't know what else I was going to do. I could... work out. Yeah, that sounded good. I could shoot a few hoops by myself, take a shower, and then come back here.

I nodded. "Yeah, I'll get out of your hair. I'll be in the gym if you need me."

"Sounds good. I'll get a simple lunch going for all the workers here and for your highness as well."

I was going to correct him, as I didn't want to be treated like royalty, but there was no point. Everyone here did it no matter how many times I told them otherwise. It was what they were used to.

Making my way through the corridors, I wondered how busy Chrys was today. She always got up early, but it seemed like she'd gotten up earlier than normal. I just hoped she would take a break for lunch today, as I didn't think the three stooges appreciated it when she was snacking on a sandwich while judging people. It was totally her style though.

I glanced around. The entire castle was like something out of a gothic horror story. Chrys originally convinced me that Dracula lived here, and I was freaked out for weeks. Then AJ finally let it slip that she was lying. I clenched my fist at the thought of him. It was his fault all this had happened—he had betrayed Chrys for eternal life. Now he was in Tartarus where he would get what he deserved.

The castle scenery grew on me, mainly because it was pretty cool to be living in a castle that looked like Dracula's. It was even more fun to sneak around when

Hades was here with the fear of getting caught. It was like a horror movie.

I made it to the gym and grabbed a basketball and began picking random places to shoot from. This was a lot more fun when Chrys had more time and we would dick around, playing different sports such as soccer or tennis. It was one of the things that I was supposed to be tutoring her in because I was a great tutor from Earth. Yeah, that was a lie, and Hades totally knew it. But he let me stay around, and Chrys and I had begun to fall in love.

Well, I mean, I fell in love with her right away—she was a princess of the underworld and a goddess, so of course I was lovestruck, but I knew better than to try to woo a goddess. But somewhere down the road, she began to love me. I wondered when that had begun and if Hades realized it anywhere down the line. Although he let me stay around, he wasn't the fondest of me. I couldn't blame him. I was some kid who had died from an overdose. No parent wanted me with their daughter.

I shot about fifty hoops before getting a bit bored. I couldn't really play tennis by myself, and while I could practice some kicks for soccer, I didn't feel like it. I decided to head back and take a shower and help Luc with the ramen he was going to serve tonight, even though that wouldn't take too long. Glancing at the clock, I found it was only three in the afternoon. Time didn't make sense to me down here, but apparently it worked like it did on Earth, and I stopped questioning it. It did get a little dark at night, but most of the time it was pretty dimly lit outside as if it were like we were underwater.

Oh. Oceanus. I get it now. We were supposed to literally be under the ocean. I felt like an idiot. This was a great example of why I was not tutor material.

As I passed by a window, I saw the souls that were deemed bad, falling to Tartarus. I wondered what they had really been like when they were alive and whether they were like me and just had some bad circumstances. That was the point of Chrys's job—to make sure those who were innocent and only acting out of circumstance didn't go to the wrong place, but I had no idea what that fully entailed. It wasn't as if the world believed in the Greek gods anymore—they were all just some myth. Although, if they lived for their god and were good people, they still went to what they considered to be heaven. I wondered if they believed they were actually in heaven instead of the Asphodel Meadows. Either way, they were in paradise.

Turning my attention back to where I was going, I headed to the showers.

CHAPTER THREE

Chrys

I had some time before dinner, so I headed toward my father's old study. I stepped inside, my heart feeling as if it were being crushed. I took a deep breath and began searching yet again.

This was probably the hundredth time I had searched the room. I hadn't moved anything out of there or anything into it, as I felt there was something there that would be a clue to how to get my father back. Huntley figured I was being sentimental in why I hadn't moved my stuff in here to work on, and maybe that was part of it and the fact we had a lot of rooms I could work in, but really it was because I wanted to search this area in peace.

And that was what I was doing. Again.

It had been a while as I had given up many times in believing something was there, and I had searched for answers in his bedroom as well, but I hadn't found anything. Most of these books were just records of all the people judged, all the times Hermes came into the underworld, and any notes from Zeus or the rest of Olympus. There was a lot of hate mail from Demeter as well. I felt bad for Father in that regard—she was a bitch to me when I'd met her as well. Then there were some love letters from my mother when they first got married. I tried not to gag on those.

But there was nothing old enough to refer to Tartarus.

Tartarus had been created by Zeus to seal away the Titans they'd fought, including their father Kronos. It also housed any evil soul, human, god, or demigod that died. Then the other afterlife worlds were created— Asphodel Meadows for the humans and Elysium for the gods and demigods—and Hades was to rule them all in the underworld. People acted like it was a horrible realm to rule, but it was actually quite nice as there weren't that many people to deal with, except the dead, and one didn't have to deal with nosy gods. Excluding Hermes randomly showing up, of course.

There were a few gods who lived in the underworld, but they were off doing their own business. There was Charon, who rowed people to their designated afterlife if they weren't going to Tartarus, Makaria, Hypnos, Morpheus, Nyx, Hekate, Thanatos, the Fates, and the Furies. So there were a few gods down here, but most kept to themselves. I hadn't seen most of them in months, other than Charon. He was the only one who didn't keep to himself.

I began pulling books off the shelves and flipping through them to double-check their contents before putting them back. Father's study was rather large, so it was going to take me at least an hour to get through a quarter of the study. I would have to come back here again to go through the rest, but I had to start somewhere.

The first shelf had books about all the residents of the underworld. I had read each and every one of them multiple times in the past two years, and none of them seemed to have powers that would help me in this quest, not to mention that they would probably try to stop me. I had to figure this out in a way that wouldn't lead to people finding out what I was doing.

The second shelf had accounting books that talked about when people were buried with coins. I wondered where those coins went, and I supposed if I really wanted to find out, I could go through all the accounting books in detail instead of simply flipping through them. It would explain why my mother always had money to spend—years of coins had started to stack up. I sighed as I finished looking through the last book. There was nothing to help me.

As I began to put the book back, I noticed there was a piece of paper stuck to the back of the bookshelf. It appeared old and worn, and I carefully peeled it off the wood and examined it.

It was definitely my father's handwriting, but I couldn't read it. It had to be in some ancient language that none of the gods used anymore or in some language that he made up. I wasn't sure which and had to find out. Perhaps I had finally found my clue, or I had simply found the warranty slip for these shelves. Either way, I needed it translated.

"Hey, what are you doing in here?" a voice said behind me.

I jumped and quickly stuck the paper in my pocket. Turning, I found Huntley standing in the doorway, his hair still a bit wet. I shrugged.

"I don't know, just looking around. I got done early today since I went to work early and decided to see if there is anything in here I should begin thinking about throwing out."

He watched me carefully for a moment. "You know you don't have to push yourself, right? This room can stay here for all eternity if you want. It's not like we need the space."

"I know. It's just that it's a lot of boring accounting. I don't need to be reminded of my father, you know?"

"I guess that's true. Whatever you want to do, I'll support you one hundred percent. You know that, right?"

I nodded. "Yup. I do. And it's why I love you so much."

Giving him a quick kiss, I turned back to the bookcase. "Anyway, I'll be in here when dinner is ready. Just come get me, okay? Looking forward to whatever you are making."

"Right. I'll do that. Get some rest too, Chrys. You deserve it."

With that, he left me working there. I thought back to what he said about supporting me one hundred percent. If he knew the truth of what I wanted to do, would he really not stop me?

I knew that if I tried to get my father out of Tartarus, the odds were that every soul, including the Titans, would be released. It was, however, a risk I was willing to make. My father didn't deserve to be down there, and if I released everything, I could just try to put it all back. No harm done. At least that was what I was praying for.

Hours passed, and I didn't find anything else like the note I'd found. Apparently it was the only note that had anything in the language my father wrote in. I knew every human language—I had been tutored by dead humans all my life after all, and this wasn't anything like any of them. It had to be the language before humanity.

Which meant I had to find an old god who could read it.

Luckily there were some old gods here in the

underworld. I would have to travel to Maka's first, as she was the one person I trusted most. If she didn't know, she could point me in the right direction without asking too many questions. I could explain that I thought it was a note to me from my father. Most people would buy that. I would feel bad about lying to her, however, but I had to do this for my father. I didn't have a choice.

Heading to the dining hall, I inhaled a wonderful scent filling the corridors. My mouth watered. It definitely smelled like ramen. Huntley loved making food from all over the world, and I was glad I was able to convince the chef to teach him. At first he was hesitant, as Huntley still appeared like, well, Huntley. He was a punk through and through, but that was what I liked about him. He wasn't afraid of being himself, and that was rare. He and the chef were now good friends, and Huntley was getting pretty good at cooking everything.

I burst through the doors. "I smell ramen!"

Huntley laughed as he was dishing out some of the sides to place on top. "You always did love ramen."

"Of course, there is so much you can do with it, especially with the toppings. Each time you have it, it's a different experience."

"That's definitely true. Well, I hope you like it. I added a little more spice this time, and we put in some braised pork belly and egg and of course bean sprouts and corn."

My mouth was watering a lot now. Huntley took out the chair for me, and I grabbed some of the chopsticks and began slurping down the meal.

It was perfect. I added a little garlic oil on top, because I loved garlic and because it brought out the flavor of the pork belly. After we were finished, I leaned back, patting my stomach.

"That was delicious. I don't think I can eat another bite."

Huntley raised an eyebrow. "Not even ice cream with caramel and soy sauce?"

"Well, there's always room for ice cream."

He laughed as he went into the kitchen to grab the treat. I glanced down at my bowl. That was truly an amazing meal. Huntley could pick up a lot of skills if he kept to it. I wondered what else he would be able to do with all the time in the world on his side.

And how long would it take for him to realize eternity was a miserable existence?

I knew I shouldn't be thinking about our future so negatively, but when I looked back at my parents, I couldn't help myself. They used to be in love like he and I were, and then it all fell apart. Granted, I didn't have to deal with Demeter and all those bitches in Olympus, but Huntley was human. Would he realize that paradise was waiting for him and eventually leave me?

And would I be able to deal with that?

CHAPTER FOUR

Huntley

Last night Chrys had seemed happy. I was glad I was able to make her smile with the ramen, but when I'd come back with the ice cream, that mood seemed to be swept away again. I tapped my forehead with my fist. What could I do to make all this better? What could I do to make her truly smile again?

She was a goddess— she had all the time in the world to mourn. I wasn't used to the idea of centuries passing, so I tried my best to be patient. I had been in the underworld for a few years now, but I still wasn't even technically thirty in human years. Time was starting to go by faster—I noticed that at least. Was this what it felt like for all humans, or was it just because I worked with gods now?

I tried to think back to the last time I had an actual conversation with a human. I couldn't remember—I had only interacted with gods for the past few years, if not demigods. All the humans whom I interacted with were just like bartenders, taxi drivers, and stuff like that. None of my friends were human, not that I ever had friends when I was human. All the humans I had known sucked, and I didn't like thinking about them. At least now I had friends even if they were gods.

Then it hit me—the chef was human. I sighed. I had forgotten since I had met him in the underworld. Most of the people who worked there were human. The chefs and artists were chosen by Chrys, whereas the ones who did laundry and such were humans on the border of going to Tartarus. If they worked for a decade, then they could go to Asphodel Meadows. The ones who were already going to Asphodel Meadows had their choice between there or Elysium, depending on if they had any friends or family they wanted to see in the afterlife. Most stuck to the human afterlife, but a few Chrys said had gone to Elysium.

I wondered what paradise was like. I couldn't imagine anywhere better than here, as Chrys was with me. Sure, we had to deal with day-to-day things, other gods, and all that drama, but I felt that was what kept one going, which was easier to say now that there wasn't drama. If every day was the same and perfect, would it have any meaning? Perhaps if I were in paradise, I would have a different feeling about it all.

I knew I should get up, but our bed was comfy and I didn't want to. I liked staring up at the wall, having deep thoughts. Chrys and I used to do it all the time while eating pomegranate seeds, but those days were now few and far between. I missed those days.

I just had to keep giving her time. I couldn't let all this bother me.

But it did. Perhaps tonight I would see if she wanted to have a chill session with me and listen to some music. It would make us both feel better, I believed, and she could tell me what was on her mind. There was definitely something going on with her, and she needed to open up or it would eat her up inside. It did for me when I had been human. Nothing good ever came when bottling up. One had to find the perfect person to tell, however, and those people could be rare.

I took a deep breath and finally got up. I didn't feel like cooking today and decided it would be a good day to take a stroll and see what was going on with the rest of the castle. Sometimes I would go weeks without going to one whole section of the castle. It was strange living somewhere so large. I told myself it was like living in a town, and sometimes you just didn't travel in certain directions because you didn't need to.

Changing into some comfy clothes, which was just a band T-shirt—Falling in Reverse—jeans, and Chucks, I headed to the kitchen to let Luc know what I was up to for the day. He told me I needed a break anyway, and I wandered off in a random direction.

I passed by Hades's old study. I had a lot of memories of that place, as it was where I found the pomegranate seeds. It was also where Hades gave me the Lethe vial to give to Prometheus. I was still really pissed at him for betraying me and everything and kidnapping Chrys like he did. Pothos and Mel were supposed to alert me if they ever found him again, but so far they hadn't found any clues. He was good at hiding, I gave him that. I didn't feel like taking my wrath out on Apollo, mainly because we needed the sun and he was just going along with it for fun. And he scared me.

As I moved farther through the castle, flashbacks of when Gwen, AJ, and I used to hang out and play games, talk about the world, and hide from Persephone came flooding back. I hated AJ, but I didn't have many memories of this place without him. That would change, of course, but at the moment they were still my favorite memories. We used to be so carefree back then —before shit hit the fan. I wished we could go back to those days.

Was this what it felt like to become an adult? I had hoped to skip that part being dead and all, but alas, here I was, looking at my past like I could change it.

That made me laugh a little. I was finally understanding what some of my teachers were referring to—at least ones who actually cared to teach their students. In the area I grew up in, not many teachers liked their students, but some stood up for us. Some wanted us to be successful. I didn't believe it was a teacher's job to make sure everything was fine, but at the same time it could mean so much to a kid. It meant something to me those few times even if in the end I couldn't be saved.

Maybe it was a bad idea to wander and let my mind go where it wanted. It brought back sad memories I didn't want to deal with. At least now I had Chrys— someone who loved me and would never leave me. I would cherish her forever.

Deciding it would be better to let off some steam by shooting hoops and working out instead of wandering like this, I headed toward the gym. Working out created endorphins, right? At least that's what *Legally Blonde* taught me.

The day went on, and after dinner, Chrys and I headed back to our room for the evening. We got halfway there when I stopped her.

"Hey, I have an idea. How about we have some pomegranate seeds?"

Her eyes perked up for a moment at the idea, but then the brightness flickered away. "I don't know. It feels wrong to me to get high like that when I have so many duties, you know? I feel like I would betray Father in not always being at my most alert. What if something happened while I was intoxicated?"

She had a point there. I grabbed her hand. "But think about it like this—he had them stashed away in his room because he was using them when he was ruler of the underworld. You really would just be doing exactly what he was when he was alive."

I watched as she started pondering that thought. Perhaps I had gotten to her.

"Fine. But only for tonight. I don't want to regularly use them anymore."

I grinned. "Sure thing. I'm not even sure how many are left. I suppose if I tried, I could figure out where he was getting them from."

She laughed. "I bet you could. You found them in his office in the first place. You really know how to snoop."

"Yes, I do. Now, the question is, where do you want to go with it?"

She bit her lip. "Maybe my old room? Haven't been back there in a while."

I nodded. "Sounds like a plan. Let's go."

When Chrys took over the underworld, she procured herself a larger and nicer room. Even though she was a princess and a goddess, she used to have a sort of small room like that in a typical suburban house. I had asked her why, and she said it just felt nicer and homey. She had the entire castle technically and could go wherever she wanted, so why would she need such huge things? It made sense to me.

We arrived at her room and opened it to find it exactly how she left it two years ago. It felt like we were coming back home from college or something. The posters were still on the walls of bands I had introduced her to. I grinned at the fond memories in there.

I pulled out two seeds from my pocket and gave her one. She took it as she flopped on the beanbag chair. It was fun to see a goddess relax in one—it was as if they were actually human after all.

Taking my own seed, I sat down on the ground and let the amazing drug take over. It was unlike anything I had ever taken before—uplifting yet calming and didn't cause that craving like all the other drugs did. I could still think straight, but everything was so vivid. I bet one would make a killing off this in the human world, not that I would ever do that.

"So, Chrys, what has been on your mind?"

She let out a laugh. "What, did you think getting me drugged would get me to talk?"

When she put it that way, I felt a little bad. Yeah, that

was what I was doing, wasn't it? Really I just wanted her to be happy, but I'd probably gone about this the wrong way.

"Sorry, I didn't mean to… I just wanted to see you smile again. I love you. You know that, right?"

Chrys leaned forward and smiled at me. Her beautiful brown eyes watched me, and her hair was messy in a way that made me smile. "I know. I love you too. I'm sorry I have been distant. I just haven't accepted the fact that he's gone. I never believed I would have to rule the underworld like this. I'm adjusting, and it will take some time. Bear with me, okay?"

I nodded as I took her hand and kissed it. "Of course. I'll do anything for you."

She kissed me gently on the lips. "Thank you. That means the world to me—more than you could ever imagine."

No, I thought, *you mean more to me than you could ever know.*

CHAPTER FIVE

Chrys

"Hey, Huntley. After what you said about needing a break to process everything, I decided that I probably should go visit Maka."

I knew Huntley meant that I needed to open up to him more, but with what I carried in my pocket, that was probably not going to happen. Although he said he would support me in everything I did, I didn't believe he would agree to potentially releasing the Titans.

Although neither would Maka.

"Oh, okay. That works since the guys are coming down tonight and we have a D&D session."

I nodded. Hermes, Pothos, Ares, and Huntley all had a Dungeons & Dragons game going on. Pothos had found out about the game, and they were all hooked. I wasn't quite sure how they convinced Ares to play, and I was not going to question it. They had fun, and that was all that mattered.

"Maka and I go way back, so she definitely can help me figure out what I need. And she has some nice tea blends. Perhaps she can make me one to feel a bit better." That was all definitely true—especially the tea part.

"Oh yeah, I forgot about that. Ask her to make me some tea as well. I would love to try more of her blends."

I smiled. "Will do. I'll see you later tonight then?"

"Probably late, yeah. You know how D&D goes."

I did. They sometimes got really into it and played for hours. Sometimes I wouldn't see the others leaving until the early morning. We were all gods, so it wasn't like we got that tired, but still, even Ares was having fun. I would have to try it someday.

Huntley gave me a kiss and headed toward the kitchen to prepare snacks and dinner for his guests. I changed into a cute dress—Maka preferred that sort of thing, so I wanted to be on her good side—and headed out the door.

I had alerted Charon that I needed a ride. I thought about just going on my own, but last time I did that, I thought I was going to die. Charon was at the ready, and I climbed aboard the gondola.

"Queen Chrysanthemum, it is a pleasure."

I took in a deep breath, then let out a sigh. I could tell this was going to be a long trip. I leaned back and closed my eyes.

"So, I have to tell you this joke." He began laughing before even saying it. I had a feeling watching him tell it was funnier than the actual joke.

"Okay, okay. So two elephants walk into a bar." He started to chuckle again, which made me laugh.

"The bartender asks what would you two like? And the first elephant says a martini." More laughter. I shook my head.

"And the bartender says okay, what about you? And the second elephant says…" Charon moved his hand in front of his face and acted like an elephant with the sound and everything. He laughed so hard he almost fell into the river.

"That's a good one, Charon," I said. It was funny, but it was a lot more entertaining to watch him tell it.

"I thought you would appreciate it. You seem a little down."

I felt a little warmer, knowing he was just trying to make me smile. "Thank you, Charon. It definitely made me laugh."

"I know, I'm amazing. Now, how is your mom doing? I haven't seen her in a while."

That was because she abandoned this place the moment she no longer had to come here. "I think she's catching up with her mom."

"Ah. Demeter. That goddess is such a bitch. She may be the goddess of fertility, but she sure has an angry side. I'm glad your father was able to stand up to her. It would have been sad to see his heart broken."

Charon had been serving my father since before my mother was in the picture. I had forgotten about that. I bit my lip, wondering if I should ask him about the note. I was about to when I realized he never could keep a secret, so word would quickly get out about what I was doing. I had to wait for Maka.

"Charon, what was my father like before he met Persephone?"

"Hmm, that was so long ago it is hard to completely recall, but your father was definitely a recluse. He didn't like dealing with any of Olympus and was a workaholic."

"You described my father when he was with my mother, not before."

He laughed. "Yeah, but it was different. When Persephone came, he was a lot happier and there was a certain glee in his step. He stopped pushing all of us away and started throwing more events, dinners, and the like."

"Then I came along and he had to stop all that so I wasn't discovered."

"No, all the underworld knew you existed. We were sworn to secrecy. Everyone just became more and more busy with the increase in numbers of humans, and the rest was history. Your father, up until his death, was still happy because of both your mother and you. You just had to know him well enough to see it."

That was true. He didn't like showing his emotions.

Charon went on. "He loved you. Before then he didn't know how to love, or at least I don't think so. His father had tried to destroy him and then was sent here away from everyone. Although he says he doesn't like the other gods, I can't help spectacle if deep down he felt left out by them all."

I wondered if Charon was right. I had always believed he despised them, but what if that was just how he coped with being down here by himself?

The rest of the trip went by smoothly, although Charon did keep telling embarrassing stories of when I was a kid. Apparently I was self-conscious about my tongue size and didn't know what a kiss was. I felt so thankful when I saw Maka waiting for me on the pier. I ran straight to her and wrapped my arms around her.

"Thank goodness. Save me from this scary man," I whispered to her.

She laughed. "Leave poor Charon alone. He means well."

"He said that you secretly dye your hair."

Her face went serious. "I'll kill him."

We both started laughing as I grabbed my stuff and thanked Charon for the ride. Maka's home was just as I remembered it. The scent of herbs filled the entire house. Little trinkets and plants littered the areas, and the sofa set was covered in a floral design. The walls were painted a light green, and the hardwood flooring was dark but fading just a tad.

"Sit down. I'll bring out some tea and sweets, then you can tell me why you wanted to come out here this time." She disappeared into the kitchen.

I called out to her. "Perhaps I just wanted to visit my friend!"

"Sure you did!"

She knew me all too well. After a few moments, she brought out a plate of cheese that was covered in flowers and herbs with some seeded crackers. She poured a light-colored tea into two different cups that were both covered in floral designs. She really liked her flowers.

"What type of tea is this?" I asked as I sniffed. It smelled very floral.

"It is jasmine tea. It's relaxing but gives a bit of energy. Take a sip and see what you think."

I took a sip. She was indeed right—it was calming. It was sweet too and didn't need anything added to it. I set the cup down as it was still a little hot.

Maka set her own cup down. "Now, tell me, how have you been?"

I gave her a look. "What do you think?"

She placed her hand on my knee. "I know it is hard. You are strong for taking up his duties. Not many could take his place."

"I don't want to take his place. I just want him back."

"All things come to an end, Chrys. Your father knew this, and that is why he prepared you to judge the souls of the dead."

I slammed my fist against the coffee table, making the cups shake a bit. "But it's not just that he's dead— he's in Tartarus! He should be in Elysium! He doesn't deserve to suffer!"

She was quiet for a moment. She picked up her cup and took a sip. "All the underworld knows this. We are heartbroken. We don't like seeing our king suffering either, but there is nothing we can do."

This was as good of a time as ever to show her what I needed translated. I pulled the paper out of my dress pocket. "Can you read this?"

She took the paper and examined it. "What is this?"

"I found it in my father's study. I'm just curious what it says."

She examined it a little longer, then handed it back. "I can't read it. It was the language used before the underworld even came to exist. We will have to find someone else to read it."

I was surprised she didn't ask more questions about it and how I was going to use the information on it. I put the paper back in my pocket and took a sip of tea.

"Please don't tell me we are going to go see them again."

She grinned. "But you love the Fates so much."

I sighed. I really didn't. They were a little scary and intimidating. And the oldest one really creeped me out, not to mention I felt as if she was the one responsible for my falling into Tartarus a couple years back. Thank goodness Hermes was there to save me.

"Fine. If they are the only ones who will help me, I'll do it."

"That's the spirit. Let's finish up these snacks, and we can head over there. Now I'm curious what the paper says."

I nodded as I sliced some of the cheese spread onto a cracker. "You know, the meals you make remind me a lot of what Circe made."

She frowned. "Circe and I don't exactly get along."

Duly noted. I reminded myself not to bring that up again. But they really were similar. Perhaps that was why they didn't get along.

CHAPTER SIX

Huntley

I always hurried out to the balcony when Hermes was to arrive because he always put on a show. Also because it was fun to see him carrying Ares on his back and Pothos like a girl in his arms. Pothos, of course, was never ashamed of being carried in such a way and always posed like he was Marilyn Monroe or something, but Ares always had a scowl on his face.

Then again, that was just how his face appeared.

Hermes landed, and the two other gods jumped off him. He posed like a hero. "We are here for the Dungeons & Dragons! Even if there haven't been any dungeons or dragons."

"No dungeons or dragons yet," Pothos added. "Not my fault your group keeps getting sidetracked."

Hermes pointed at him. "Hey, that is your fault for including dino races. You think we weren't going to get sidetracked wanting to ride dinos?"

He had a point there. I really wanted to ride them too. Hermes ended up winning, and Ares lost. I had never seen him so pissed. It was epic.

I clapped my hands together. "Well, Chrys is gone for the evening, so we have the place to ourselves, not that that really matters since she stayed clear of you all. But I made some jalapeño bites, spanakopita pockets, chicken wings, guac and queso, and loaded potato skins."

Pothos slapped my back. "Huntley, why couldn't you have picked up this hobby when you were living with me? Your food is amazing."

"Well, I didn't have a chef to teach me back then. And he did a lot of the work tonight. I just helped."

"Well, if Chrys ever kicks you out, you can most

definitely come back to live with me."

I laughed. "Thanks. I'll let her know."

We all headed toward the game room I had set up for these nights once a month, sometimes twice if we could manage it. Everyone settled in their spots, and I went to help bring in the food as Pothos set up the map and got our tokens out. I brought in all the large serving dishes and scattered them around so that everyone could pass them to whomever.

"Oh man, that smells good," Hermes said as he took in a deep breath. "You can become my wife whenever you want, Huntley, just say the word."

I blushed. "Hey, knock it off. I'm married. Chrys wouldn't appreciate you saying that."

Ares was stuffing his face with the spanakopita already, along with the chicken wings. It made me a little happy that he enjoyed my food. Who else could say that the god of war liked their cooking?

"Well then, should we get this game started?" Pothos asked as he picked up a D20.

I took a seat and began munching on some guac. "Let's do this!"

Pothos began the game. "To recap, last time you were searching for a dark wizard who is bringing evil to the land. The country has had plagues, bugs, everything imaginable for the past few months. They have no water, crops, and are going to perish unless you can find what is causing all this. You were given the information that a strange man was seen, heading to the mountains before all the disasters hit, and that is where you are heading. You are still five days away."

Hermes glanced at Ares and me. "I say we keep heading toward the mountain. If we can find a nice river, we could move a little faster. I roll for investigation." He rolled the die. It was a two. "Fuck. Five total."

Pothos laughed. "Yeah, so, you see trees. And ground. And like, plants exist."

Ares stuffed some chips in his mouth. "I thought you were supposed to be some genius bard."

"Well, it doesn't help that my dice hate me!" He snapped his fingers, and a new set of dice appeared. "There. That's better."

Pothos held out his hand. "Let me see those."

"And if I refuse?"

"I'll consider all your rolls to be ones, and you will die quickly."

Hermes sighed. "Fine." He snapped his fingers and

the dice disappeared.

"Yup, I knew it. Trick dice."

"Well he is a bard and trickster god," Ares said. "What did you expect?"

"I expected the god of athletic contests to be a better sport."

"Ha! Joke's on you. I'm also the god of thievery and cunning. I just do what I want."

I wondered if he and Loki were really the same god but different stories. I could definitely see Hermes doing most of what Loki did in the stories I read about when I was younger.

I picked up my dice. "As a warlock, I roll investigation so I can see if I can find a river." I rolled my dice. "Twelve plus my modifier, so sixteen."

Pothos checked his papers. "You hear some water in the distance ahead of you. Do you proceed?"

I glanced at the others. They all nodded. "Yes, we do."

We headed toward the water and used our collapsible rafts and made our way to the mountain via the river. As our characters got closer to the mountain, the harsher the water became.

Pothos glanced at his sheet. "So do you get out or are

you going to proceed?"

I took a bite of my chicken wing. It was BBQ flavored, one of my favorite sauces. "When Pothos says it like that, I feel like he's up to something. Should we get out?"

Ares narrowed his eyes. "Or is there something in the forest, and he's trying to get us to be attacked by that?"

Hermes waved his hand. "It's both. Pothos is sadistic and can read our thoughts. He knows with how chaotic we are, that he needs to plan for both."

"So should we stay?" I asked.

"Yes. It's getting us there faster."

Pothos grinned. "Roll for initiative."

We battled the rapids, then merfolk, then some kind of river shark, which I still didn't think existed, and that was all before we camped for the night. We were at the base of the mountain now and shaved off five days of walking with the boat ride. And we leveled up from our fight. I quickly added the numbers from a level 3 warlock half elf to a level 4 and increased my ability score. I added it to intelligence because we definitely needed it in this game. Ares just focused on strength for his half-orc fighter, which wasn't a surprise. Hermes had a human bard, which was also not a surprise. He tried to sleep with as many townsfolk as he could. He was also clever but didn't ever roll well.

"It's dark now—do you all want to take a long rest before you start to scale the mountain?"

I nodded. "I think that is smart. We can trade off who is keeping watch. Then we will be back to full health, and Hermes and my character will have their spell slots back."

Pothos jotted some notes down. I always hated it when he did that. "All right. Who is up first?"

Ares grunted. "I'll stay awake first. I have the least damage."

Ares did know how to fight, I gave him that. He rarely got hurt bad, not to mention he rolled well. I wished I could roll as well as he usually did.

Wait, did that mean Ares was using trick dice? Pothos never checked his dice, just Hermes's. Did he not think Ares would cheat, or was he too afraid to ask? It was probably the latter, or at least it would be for me.

"Roll for investigation."

Ares rolled. "Twenty-two total."

"Everything is fine and dandy. It's a nice night, and it seems the merfolk are all gone, and there are no monsters nearby due to the evil aura tonight."

That was good to hear. I did not want to go into battle again. Although I knew what it was like to fight for real, I couldn't help but be nervous even in a game. You never knew what was going to happen and whether you would have to make a new character. That always sucked.

It was my time to watch for the night. I also rolled a high number and didn't find anything out of the ordinary.

Pothos flipped through the papers he had. "How about we take a little break and then start the next day? I need to make sure everything is in order."

We all got up and stretched. Most of the food was gone. I figured I would wait until our next break to grab the desserts. I had made some cheesecake bites, brownies, macaroons, and orange-and-white-chocolate cookies. Just the thought of them made my stomach hurt.

Hermes stepped up to me. "So, where did Chrys go for the evening?"

"Oh, Maka's. They haven't visited in quite some time. I figured it would be good for her to just chill for a bit."

Hermes nodded. "Yeah, that light in her eye hasn't come back, has it? I don't blame her, but I also don't like seeing her like this."

"I just wish there was more I could do for her. I feel helpless."

Hermes patted my back. "You are doing everything you can. You have made a great husband—greater than any that I have ever seen. You two belong together. She just needs time. Give her a century or so."

That sounded like a long time, but it was nothing to these gods. Perhaps I thought she was taking a while because she was human, but really it was like a few days to her since she could live so long.

"Right. I guess I'll do that."

CHAPTER SEVEN

Chrys

I didn't want to be back there, but I also really wanted to know what the note said. This was all a price I was willing to pay to learn the truth about Tartarus. Or, at least, potentially about Tartarus. For all I knew, it could have just been a recipe for the best cake in the world, which wouldn't be a terrible thing, but then I would be at another dead end for getting my father back.

Maka knocked, and the three Fates opened the door.

All of them became wide-eyed when they saw me.

Yeah, this was going to be another terrible experience, but I kept up my smile.

"Her Majesty! We welcome you! Please come in. We have some candy you can eat." Atropos turned to go inside.

I was about to say I didn't want any candy when Maka elbowed me in the side. She grinned.

"We would be honored."

The two of us stepped inside. Bright floral wallpaper covered the interior. Everything had flowers on it in a way that was obnoxious, unlike Maka's place, which was subtle. Here, even the plastic-covered couch was covered in all sorts of colored blooms with a pink background. It made me want to vomit.

One of the Fates, Lakhesis, set down a tray of strange-looking candy. "Here, eat!"

I took one and sniffed it. It just smelled like sugar. After watching Maka eat it, I popped it in my mouth. It was sweet and softer than I thought it would be.

Klotho took a seat and folded her hands gently in her lap. "Well, what brings you here?"

Maka nodded to me. I pulled out the paper. "I was wondering if you were able to read this and tell me what it says. I found it in my father's study."

Klotho snagged it before the other two could make a grab for it. I just prayed that they wouldn't rip it as they fought over it. Lakhesis and Atropos stuck their heads next to Klotho. They all had a concerned look on their faces.

"Mm-hmm. Yes."

I perked up. "What is it?"

"It isn't a language, per se. It's an old code used by primordial gods."

I glanced over to Maka. She seemed as surprised as I was. I turned back to them. "Can you read it?"

Klotho brought it closer to her face, as if that would make it easier. "No. I cannot. Perhaps Mother can."

"Are you all talking about me behind my back again?" Themis appeared out of thin air like she did the time before. I felt as if my heart was skipping a beat. Was she going to figure out what I wanted to do? Was she going to stop me? Or would she send me to Tartarus again?

Klotho handed her the paper. "Her majesty brought this paper. She says she found it among Hades's stuff. Can you decipher it?"

Themis took the paper from her daughters and

adjusted her glasses. "Ah. I haven't seen this code in a long time."

I grabbed at the fabric of my dress. "So you can read it?"

"No. I cannot. But I have seen this code before and I know who can." She handed the paper back to me. "But the question is, what are you going to do with it?"

My eyes widened. If she couldn't read it, how would she know what it was about? "I... I just want to know what it says because it was in my father's stuff. If it was coded, then perhaps it is important. It could be a letter to me for all I know. It's just important to me, that's all."

Maka patted my leg, and I tried not to burst into tears. I felt as if something was wrong with me—as if I couldn't be whole again unless I knew what was on the paper. What if she didn't tell me? What if she knew what the information entailed and wouldn't give me the name of the person who could read it? It wouldn't matter, I supposed, as I could at least find someone who could read it. I just would run into the same problem of them not wanting to tell me the truth.

"Well, I can fathom a daughter wanting to understand her father more now that he is gone. But the person you will need to ask isn't the best god to deal with. He tends to stay away from god matters and does his own thing —which includes corrupting humans and drugs and whatnot."

I furrowed my brow. Didn't that sound like all the gods?

Maka asked, "You don't mean who I think you mean, do you?"

Themis nodded as she took a seat. "Aether, my grandfather."

I tried my hardest to keep track of the genealogy of all the gods, but I lost track long ago, not to mention gods married whomever, and sometimes gods just came into existence.

"Where is he?" I asked.

Maka shook her head. "Sweetie, I think you should let this go. Aether isn't someone you should get involved with."

I turned to her. "But I need to know what this says. What if it was a message for me?"

She bit her thumb. I had never seen her so distressed. "Aether is god over the air above the sky—heavenly air, so to speak. However, the humans began worshipping the spirit through drugs, including opium.

Since he realized that he could get humans obsessed with him through drugs like that, he has been controlling all the drug businesses around the world. Even if you found him, it isn't likely that you will get any answers from him. At least not without a price."

The more I heard about Aether, the less I wanted to get involved. I opened up the paper again to look at my father's handwriting. There had to be a reason this was hidden behind a book and stuck to the wood of the bookcase. It wouldn't just be some random note—especially if it used a code only the primordial gods used.

What was going on? Why was this never easy?

"Unfortunately I don't know his whereabouts at the moment, so I can't help you either way," Themis explained. "But I must warn you, as Maka said, he is not the best company to get involved with. All his children are the reason the world is in such chaos and why there will always be evil. He brought daimons into existence."

That was the first I had heard of it. How did I not know? Why was this never taught to me? Were you hiding Aether from me, Father? Because of what he could do?

I finally nodded. "I understand. I won't go looking for him. Thank you for helping me."

"Not to change topics, but you have to admit." She folded her arms in front of herself. "My prophecy of you changing Olympus and the world was correct. And you ended up with the boy you loved, yes? Don't feel you have to praise me on my excellent fortune-telling."

It did come true, but at what cost?

"Yes, you were spot on," I finally said. "And Huntley and I are happily married."

"Well, that part I didn't know since I was never invited to the wedding."

I laughed a little. "After everything in Olympus, we didn't have a ceremony. But if we did, you would have been one of the first people I would have sent an invitation to."

"Well, good. That's how it should be."

Klotho smacked her mother. "How can you be so rude? You knew how weddings in the underworld are usually done in secret. It's so romantic, isn't it? Like father, like daughter, sneaking those pomegranates to their loved ones."

"Yeah, it was something like that." Technically, Huntley was the one who'd found them first, but I didn't feel like correcting them. There didn't seem to be a point. "Anyway, I believe Maka and I should be going. She has a lot of work to do, and I wanted to get back before it gets late."

Before I could stand up to leave, Themis grabbed my wrist and pulled me in to whisper in my ear.

"That paper you have there, it's dangerous. Don't be stirring up any trouble, you hear me? There are a lot of dangerous things lurking in the dark—things that shouldn't be let outside. But you would know that, wouldn't you?"

I nodded. "Yeah, because someone pushed me in."

She laughed but didn't comment on what I said. "Now get going. You young folk are always so busy. You should try to take more breaks."

"Yeah, yeah," Maka commented. "That's what happens when you are goddesses. All work and no play, right Chrys?"

"Right."

CHAPTER EIGHT

Huntley

"Firebolt!" I cast my cantrip since I had run out of spell slots.

"Roll for damage." Pothos scribbled more notes.

I rolled and grinned widely. "Ten."

More scribbling. What, was he writing a novel or something? He brought his hands together.

"You see the dragon lord start to waver. He reaches out toward the heavens, calling out a name, and suddenly he collapses."

I shot my fist up in the air. "Yay! I did it!" And with only four hit points to spare. I thought I was a goner.

"You mean we did it." Ares folded his arms in front of himself. "I do believe we all attacked him with everything we had."

"Right, yeah. But I gave the final blow."

Ares glared at me but didn't say anything more.

Hermes grabbed his D20. "I roll investigation to see if I can loot his stuff." He rolled. "Sixteen."

"You find a key on his person and chest in the corner," Pothos said.

The three of us looked at each other. I shrugged. "I want to know what's in the box."

Hermes nodded. "As do I."

"Your funeral," Ares commented, but he didn't protest.

Hermes turned to Pothos. "I open it and jump back."

"You find that there are three treasures. A bow and arrow that always hits its target, a lyre that can double any sleep attack, and a warlock book full of dark, lost spells."

"Well," Ares began. "I know what I am taking. Any of you try to take that bow from me, I'll stab you in real life."

"The lyre is mine! I call dibs!"

I, of course, wanted the book. "I'm excited for some dark spells."

Pothos began gathering papers and passed them out. "Well, here are the stats for each item and how much it is worth if you ever need to sell it. Keep that in your folders, and we shall meet again in a month."

"Sounds good," I said as I started gathering my dice and then stacking the plates. We definitely ate a lot. It seemed gods could pack a lot in their stomachs, but I was glad that they enjoyed the meals I helped make. So far they hadn't disliked anything I'd chosen.

"Did you all just end your game?" A voice came from the doorway.

I turned to find that Chrys was back. She was in a cute purple floral dress, which looked good on her but was definitely not something she normally wore.

"Yup, we defeated the evil guy trying to destroy the land too," I said with a bit of a grin.

"Well, good for you. I wouldn't have expected anything else."

"He almost died," Pothos added. "He lost the most hit points of everyone."

I gave him a look. "Did you really have to say that?"

He nodded. "I did. I couldn't let you look that good to your wife."

I rolled my eyes and turned to Chrys. "So, how was Maka?"

"Good. We talked and had some tea." She held up a bag. "I brought some back."

"I can't wait to try it. Perhaps I'll make a whole tea platter to match the taste."

She smiled. "That would be lovely."

Hermes stepped up to her and gave her a big hug. "It is great to see you, Chrys. I hope you are doing well."

"As well as I can. But I'm glad I caught you before you left. I have something to talk to you about."

He raised an eyebrow. "Oh?"

She and Hermes went into the hallway. It was clear that whatever it was, none of us were supposed to hear, but that made me want to know even more. I glanced over at Pothos who was frowning.

"What is it?" I asked.

He shook his head. "Nothing. Don't worry about it. I would just keep an eye on Chrys if I were you. She seems to be pretty distraught still about Hades."

And I couldn't blame her. He didn't deserve to go to

Tartarus as he used to be king of this land. He was the nicest god I knew. "I will. I'm just not sure what to do."

"It will take time, but just make sure she doesn't do anything stupid, all right? I mean, she's a powerful god, and she really could make a mess of things."

"Again," Ares commented. "I mean, she did almost destroy everything. Just make sure she doesn't break anything again."

I wanted to make a snarky comment back, but he had a point. She did almost destroy everything, but it wasn't completely her fault. Zeus had provoked her.

"I'll make sure she's fine here. I mean, I have these delicious meals going down here."

Pothos laughed. "That you do. Really I come here for your cooking rather than the D&D session."

Ares grunted. "Same."

Hermes stepped back into the room with Chrys. He had a concerned look on his face and Chrys appeared to be thinking. Hermes turned to Pothos and Ares.

"Shall we head back? It's getting late."

Pothos and Ares nodded as they gathered their things.

"It was fun having you all," I said as I walked them out. "Looking forward to our next campaign."

Pothos grinned. "It's going to be legendary. I have

been working on it already for weeks."

"Oh goodie," commented Ares. "I can't wait to see what trouble you have cooked up for us."

I wasn't sure if he was being sarcastic or if he really did like fighting. It was probably the latter.

Hermes pulled me to the side. "Watch over Chrys for me, all right? I'm not sure what she is up to."

"What did she talk to you about?" I asked.

"I'm not allowed to say. But just make sure she doesn't do anything rash, okay?"

I nodded. "Of course."

He patted the side of my arm. "Well, until next time." He turned to the others. "Who wants to be carried like a princess?"

Pothos quickly answered. "Not it!"

Ares clenched his fist. "Damn you."

"Hey, it's your turn."

Pothos climbed on Hermes's back, and Hermes picked up Ares like a princess. I held back my laughter as I knew he would kill me if I even chuckled. I watched as they flew up and headed out. I had offered to give them the rings that Persephone had made for all her suitors, but none of them wanted to deal with Charon, and Hermes got out of the underworld a bit faster.

I let out a sigh as I knew I would miss them until the next time they came. Although I loved it down here, I had to admit I got lonely at times. At least I had some people to interact with, but they weren't as close as Pothos and I had become.

Turning toward the castle, I found Chrys in her father's study. I knocked on the door and she jumped.

"Oh hey, Huntley."

Books were moved from the shelves as if she were looking for something.

"What are you doing?"

She shrugged. "Just trying to see if Father left anything I needed while ruling the underworld—that's all."

I slowly nodded. "Right. And what did you talk to Hermes about?"

"Oh, I just wanted to know whether Prometheus had been found. He still hasn't."

That was a lie—a lie she had ready. "Look, I want him caught and tried as much as you do, but he is one sneaky bastard. Eventually he will turn up."

She shrugged. "I really don't blame him for what he did. He sort of saved me in some ways and risked his life."

"So he could use you against Zeus."

She shrugged again. "All the gods seem to use each other. He just isn't any different."

I disagreed with that. I had lived with him for months, and the way he crafted everything was just plain devious. But it was her decision. I just would get a few punches in before she let him go.

"Well, did you find anything in here?"

Her eyes widened for a moment. "What do you mean?"

So she found something and didn't want me to know. Great. "You said you were looking for any extra info about running this place. Have you found anything?"

"Oh. No. I mean, there are so many accounting records. I want to talk to my mother about it one of these days since she was the one who'd spent all the money."

"But do we really need money down here?"

"No, but if we ever wanted to visit Earth, we would need it."

"Didn't you create credit cards randomly last time we were there?"

She smiled. "I did, but the money was taken out of

these accounts. I'm not sure how much is left and how much my mother has still been spending."

Well, that made sense. "Maybe you should call for her to come down here."

"No." Chrys was quick to respond. "I... I don't want her here. Perhaps I'll have Hermes fly a letter to her, and she can respond that way."

Persephone was never the best mom, but she had done everything she could to save Chrys. I had seen her fight, and it was glorious. But she never came back to the underworld after everything, and I think that gap between mother and daughter thickened even more.

"I'm sure he could do that. He will be back in a month with the others, and you can ask then."

"Yeah. I'll do that. Did you all have fun? Did they like the treats you had picked out?"

I grinned. "They did. Pothos said if you ever kicked me out that I could be his wife."

She laughed. "Well, I'm glad you have a backup plan."

"Even Ares admitted I was a good cook. It took me by surprise."

"Now you know, if you ever piss him off, just hand him some food."

"For sure," I said as I watched her closely. Even though we were having this conversation, it was clear her mind was somewhere else. "You all right?"

She blinked. "Yeah, just tired. You know how Charon can be. It makes me very out of it after I hear him talk."

That was for sure, but this seemed different. I decided to let it go. "Well then, shall we call it a night?"

Chrys nodded. "Yeah, let's."

CHAPTER NINE

Chrys

I felt horrible about lying to Huntley, but I knew if he found out the truth, he would stop me.

He always said that if I needed anything or wanted to do anything, he would have my back. Although I knew he wasn't lying, I doubted opening the gates to Tartarus was anything he had in mind for what he would support me for.

I had asked Hermes if he knew where Aether was. He

said he wasn't sure the precise location, but he would find out and get back to me. That was two days ago, and I was still waiting on him. At least it wasn't like I didn't have anything else to do as there were always souls that needed to be judged.

What never made sense to me was that the three stooges, Minos, Rhadamanthys, and Aiakos, could also judge the souls who were on the border of Asphodel Meadows and Tartarus, but I was supposed to be here to help them. If they just did their job without supervision, then I could work on other matters, such as trying to figure out how to open the gates to Tartarus. I sighed as Cerberus grabbed the victim by the collar and pulled him down to Tartarus.

"Next!" I yelled out.

I wondered what these souls thought of me. Who were they expecting to be on the throne of the underworld? It wasn't as if many believed in the Greek gods any longer. Huntley had told me a bit about the religion of his area. Did they believe me to be Lucifer? Or did they think I was some other demon sending them to hell? It was especially interesting to have heavily religious people have to be judged since they claimed they believed in this so-called Christ so all their sins should have been cleaned before they died.

Yeah, that's not how it works.

One had to actually practice morality and not just think that since they believed in such a god, they could do whatever they wanted and spit hate to everyone they met. No god I knew would take that kind of shit.

The next human was someone about the age of Huntley—a girl with reddish hair and piercings in her nose and lips. Her eyes were puffy and crying. Minos handed me her story and the list of things her life entailed.

Her story was similar to Huntley's—shitty parents, crappy town, friends who stabbed each other in the back. Sure, she wasn't the best human being, but when one dealt with only pain, it wasn't easy to do anything other than act out.

"Well, sweetie, it's your lucky day. I'm sending you to paradise. Cerberus!"

Instead of biting her clothes, Cerberus became a sweet puppy and led souls to Asphodel Meadows. The girl saw the dog and scratched each of his heads. Seeing a dog really seemed to cheer her up, and now she could forever be happy.

I clapped my hands together. "Well, I think that is all

for today. You three can deal with any stragglers. I'm going to go chill for a bit."

They fumbled with their papers as if they didn't know what to do, but I already knew they were more than capable of handling the task. Father left them to work every once in a while, not to mention when he was gone trying to find me and battling Zeus, they were in charge. I would be gone for a couple of days looking for Aether, so I wanted them to work on their own without concern as to where I was.

That just left the problem of what to tell Huntley and how to get out of the underworld.

I could use Charon's boat, but I had a feeling he would tell anyone he could where I had gone. Granted, he wouldn't know exactly where I was going, but he might tell others he took me to Earth, and the search for me would begin. No, I would have to figure out a different way to get out of here.

Perhaps I could get Hermes to take me up. He already knew I was asking for him, so it wasn't like I had to worry about another person finding out. And he was sworn to secrecy and couldn't say anything to anyone.

But first I would have to wait until Hermes could

figure out where he was and report back to me. Gods seemed as if they were hard to get rid of if you didn't want to be around them but really hard to located when you needed them most. Unfortunately for me, I was found when I didn't want to be, no thanks to AJ.

I decided to go through the last shelf in my father's study to make sure there weren't any other notes. I kept the one I'd found in my pocket so no one else could come across it, and so if I had the chance, I could leave at any given moment with it. When I had moments alone, I stared at it, trying to will it to give me the information I needed. It, of course, never worked, but one couldn't help but try.

I began taking off groups of books from the first shelf and flipping through them. In this bookcase, most of the books were fictional tales of old, such as Shakespeare and Dickens, and all who had been tutors of mine. I had found, over the years, most writers were very peculiar humans that did not fit within society. Neither did artists.

There were no notes in the back of the bookcase for the first shelf. I checked the second, which was more of the same books, and found another note. I opened it, and a glittery substance came straight at me. I coughed and tried to wipe off the pink color, but it wasn't going to disappear. I glanced at the note. It was in my father's handwriting.

I know it was you, Huntley, and I have caught you in the act. You're a dead man if I find you covered in pink.

Now there was a story. I laughed as tears began to fill my eyes. I missed him so much my heart couldn't take it any longer. I had to do something—I had to save him.

After not finding anything in the last two shelves, I headed toward the baths to clean up. As I walked, I saw Huntley coming my way. He started laughing.

"Someone got glitter bombed. I didn't think there were any more left."

I raised an eyebrow. "You knew about these?"

"Sure did. But I never set one off. I knew what was inside."

"How?"

"Punk intuition. Besides, I didn't care about paper stuff. I was always looking for those seeds."

Father should have put these in the drawers, unless he did and that was where Huntley found the others. "Did you ever find anything else?"

He shook his head. "No. Why, what are you looking for?"

"Nothing in particular. Just trying to understand my father."

"Well, from what I knew about your father, he didn't like his stuff touched. One had to be pretty clever to find anything of his that he didn't want to be found."

That was for sure. Although paper in the back of a bookcase wasn't the smartest way to go, it had been almost the same color and hard to see. The glitter bomb wasn't, however, as he wanted that to be found by Huntley. I wondered if there was anything else he had been hiding from me or if this was it. Since it was writing in primordial tongue, I figured it had to be pretty important.

"I better wash off and change. Have any idea how to get all this off of me?"

"Oil is good. We definitely have plenty of olive oil. It makes it easy to glide it off your skin with a rag."

I sighed. "Of course you would know that. Thanks, Huntley."

"My pleasure. Your father never found out I opened one. I had to act fast though, because when he figured it out, he came searching for me. Luckily AJ didn't rat me out."

I had no idea. "You are lucky to be alive still."

"That's for sure. So, yeah, oil and tape. Works wonders."

I turned and headed toward the bathroom. I would get all this stuff off and take a nice, long bath. I definitely needed it.

CHAPTER TEN

Huntley

Finding Chrys like that definitely made me chuckle. Hades had a few of those little surprises hidden away. I thought I had gotten rid of them all, but I supposed I was wrong.

Hades always knew I was sneaking into places I wasn't supposed to, but he rarely was able to catch me, so he made traps like that. It was obvious. I really didn't even have to try hard to avoid them, but one had gotten me good. It was purple and was in with the gondolas. I never expected him to hide something like that out there when I was just bored and looking through things. I knew I had to act fast or else he would send me to Tartarus.

AJ was also with me at the time, so we were able to help each other clean up and were each other's alibi. Hades, for some reason, never suspected that demigod of anything bad, even though he was definitely a worse person than I ever was. It was always like that for me, no matter where I went. I just accepted it.

Although the reason AJ went with me that time was so he could say "I told you so" when I got caught, but I was lucky in that he was close enough to the glitter bomb to be affected—otherwise he would have totally ratted me out. Lucky me.

I still wasn't quite sure what Chrys was doing in the study, but lately she had been searching a lot in there. Did she think she was going to find something? I mean, she did come across that glitter bomb. That was something. I just hoped she would find what she was looking for and finally confess what she was up to. Hermes and Pothos had said something was bothering her, and I couldn't help wonder—what could she possibly be lying to me about? Was it something serious? I doubted it could be anything small, but I didn't know. She never kept anything from me like that.

Wandering around, the feeling of helplessness wafted over me. I wasn't a god. I was just a human. What could I really do to help her? I didn't understand how everything worked yet, if I even could. I was just some human, wandering in the underworld, lucky to have her as my bride. I felt like a blessed fool and had no idea how long this fluke would last.

I mean, it wasn't easy to get to here—not after everything that had happened. But now that we were married, and we were in the clear, I felt a little out of place again. What do I do with my time? What do I do to keep all this going?

It had only been two years. I was getting ahead of myself. There would be a lot of time before anything was an issue, if we even had issues. I needed to be calm and grateful for where I was and just keep doing what I was doing.

As if I could ever be calm.

I would have to talk to Pothos and Hermes and see if they had any advice. Until then, I just needed to chill. I took a deep breath. I could do that. I could chill.

I still wasn't quite sure what I wanted to do with myself. I felt like taking a day off, cooking and working on something new, but I honestly didn't have any other hobbies. Chrys had said that she used to get tutors from different eras. Maybe I could get a tutor and learn more about something?

Shaking my head, I knew that wasn't going to work. I wasn't exactly the best at learning from someone. Teachers always hated me, and I went to a tutor once, and they gave up on me. I knew it would be different here, especially since I was like a prince, but all of it left a bad taste in my mouth.

So instead, I headed toward the library to just start learning on my own.

The library was—and I mean it in all sense of the word—huge. It was like the TARDIS or something and was larger than possible. It was bigger than any library I had ever been to or seen pictures of. Perhaps it was as large as the one on *Avatar: The Last Airbender*. It was the only one comparable in what it contained, which was everything.

I headed to the history section. The cool thing was, other than the really old stuff, everything translated into whatever language you needed it to be, so I could read all these books without having to learn another language. I would like to learn other languages, however, so I added that to my list of things to do. I just would have to figure out which one to learn first. Perhaps ancient Greek so I could know what Ares, Pothos, and Hermes were saying during the game to leave me out. Then I would respond and be like "Ha! I can understand you now!" Then they would just switch to another language, and I would have to start all over again.

Grabbing the book containing history on ancient Greece, I decided I would start there and work my way through European history and then move to another continent and so on. I didn't have to worry about tests or assignments—I could just learn.

Look at me now, assholes.

I was also the prince of the underworld, which was just strange to think about. I had been born as some poor kid living in a trailer park. I was beaten often, did drugs, got wasted, failed classes, had almost been arrested a few times, and now here I was. I wish they all could see it now. Perhaps they would when they went to the afterlife. I wasn't sure how since I didn't see many of the dead souls, but maybe they all just understood this place after they died—as if a soul knew more after it died as there was no physical world blocking its perception of reality.

Whatever—it didn't matter. I had moved on, and I could start anew. I flipped through the book and began at page one.

I'd gotten ten pages in, and my head started to hurt. Ancient Greece was first ruled in small towns or pieces of land where the aristocrats enslaved all the people and there was a lot of conflict. Why did it seem like no matter what century it was, that was always the story?

There was a lot of military advancements in Greece, which was how they defeated the Persian empire so many times. That, however, was as far as I'd gotten. There were so many Greek names that I was beginning to lose track of everything.

This was going to take forever. But I had forever, so it was fine. I was fine.

No, I still felt like an idiot. Perhaps I was trying to bite off more than I could chew. Perhaps I could just read a few pages at a time, digest it, then come back. Was that the best way to learn? It seemed like schools never had us just sit on things but kept jamming more and more information down our throats. I sighed, wondering what the best way to learn really was.

Deciding to switch gears, I turned my attention to something fun.

The problem was, I had done everything so many times now that it wasn't that fun, or at least not alone. I sighed—perhaps I should just go back and help Luc with the rest of the meals for the day. I was beginning to understand why Chrys kept AJ and me around for so long. This place was quite lonely on one's own. Or at least when you didn't have a job to do.

CHAPTER ELEVEN

Chrys

Five days had passed, and I still had no word from Hermes. I was beginning to wonder if he was going to ignore my request. Would I have to find someone else to help me? That was hard to do in this place, and if I left to go find someone, then there would be even more questions. I played with the idea of messaging my mother, but I knew that would just make matters even worse.

Just as I was about to give up, I heard Cerberus start barking hysterically. I hurried toward him to find Hermes standing on top of a bookcase.

"Get away, you stupid mutt!" Hermes exclaimed. "Sit! Go away!"

I patted Cerberus. "He's not a stupid mutt. He protects the underworld from trespassers."

"No, your father trained that dog to attack me—I know he did!"

"Because he considered you a trespasser." I looked down at Cerberus. "It's fine, Cerberus. Hermes is our friend."

Cerberus started panting and rolled over to have his belly rubbed. I peered up at Hermes.

"See, everything is fine now. No worries."

Hermes didn't budge. "Can he go outside now? I still don't trust him."

I sighed. "Fine. Cerberus, go play."

Cerberus got up and ran down the hallway. Hermes got down from the bookcase and swept himself off.

"I thought you said you taught him to stop doing that to me."

"I tried. It seems that he'd rather obey his old master."

"I see."

We were quiet for a moment, so I brought up the topic. "What did you find?"

"Aether is currently located in Hong Kong. But I have to ask, why do you need to talk to him?"

"I just want to discuss some stuff with him of my father's."

"Like what?"

I shrugged. "Just... stuff. Don't make me tell you, Hermes. It's personal."

"You'd rather talk personal stuff to a god you have never met—a god that spawned everything horrible in the world? There has to be a good reason, Chrys."

I sighed. "I really can't tell you, Hermes. It was just something I found that Father wanted me to take to him."

He frowned. "When you lie, you need to get your facts straight, you know that, right?"

"Hermes, will you please just take me to him? I can't exactly get there on my own—not without Charon telling the entire castle."

He stared at me for a long minute. I gave him the best puppy dog eyes I could. He sighed. "Fine. But you have to swear to me you aren't up to anything that will get you into trouble. You just go in and out, and we come back. Got it?"

I nodded. "Yes! I promise."

"What are you going to tell Huntley? Does he even know about this mission?"

I hesitated. "Can you not tell him? I just... I want to do this alone and fear that he might try to come with. Can we tell him we are going to go talk to my mother?"

He examined me closely. "What are you doing with Aether that you wouldn't want Huntley knowing about?"

"Hermes... Please. As the queen of the underworld, I am ordering this of you—stop asking questions."

I was the ruler of this world, and he knew that. Since he was in my domain, he had to obey my orders.

"Fine. But I'm warning you as a friend, Aether is trouble. I'll be outside his place if you need me, and if you take too long, then I'll come in and take you, all right?"

"That sounds like a plan to me. Give me an hour with him, and if I'm not out by then, come get me."

He nodded. "All right. When do you want to leave?"

"As soon as you are able. I'm free right now."

He sighed. "I have nothing better to do now that Zeus

is gone. Let's go tell Huntley we are leaving, and then we can head out."

Huntley had been frequenting the library recently, so we checked there first. As I expected, he was there, reading through a stack of books.

Hermes laughed. "What in the world are you doing, Huntley? Are you reading?"

Huntley shot a look at Hermes. "Don't make fun of me. There is a lot I don't know—I'm not as old as all of you. I just am trying to catch up."

So that was what he was doing there this past week. I felt my cheeks blush. He had never cared about all those things before. I wasn't sure if it was because he was bored or if he really did feel inadequate to us. I had a feeling it was a bit of both.

I wrapped my arms around him and kissed his cheek. "Sweetie, we are going to be gone for a bit. Hermes is taking me up to talk to my mother about a few things. Can you watch over the fort while I am gone?"

He appeared puzzled for a moment but didn't ask questions. "Sure. When will you be back?"

I shrugged. "Probably before dinner."

He nodded. "Okay. See you later then."

I kissed him on the cheek again and headed out with

Hermes.

Hermes glanced back to Huntley. "You know, he really is trying. It's hard for a human to marry a god or goddess. Eventually something bad always happens."

"Speaking from experience?"

He laughed. "Perhaps. I've been around the block a few times, mainly princesses. None of them were true love like you and Huntley have. But a lot of different gods have fallen for humans only to have something horrible happen. I'm surprised Huntley has survived this long, to be honest."

"Well, it helps when he's already dead and I am queen of the underworld."

Hermes nodded. "That it does."

We arrived at the balcony where Hermes could fly us up to Earth.

"You know, Your Majesty, it has been quite some time since I have flown you anywhere. I sort of miss it."

I raised an eyebrow. "What, is flying with Ares and Pothos not the same?"

"No. It's not. I'd rather carry a beautiful woman in my arms than those two brutes."

He picked me up, and I wrapped my arm around his

neck. "I wouldn't call Pothos a brute. But Ares must be heavy."

"That he is. I definitely have been building up strength by carrying them both. At least I have that going for me."

"Oh, believe me, Hermes, you don't look a day over one thousand."

"Why, thank you, m'lady."

"Speaking of which, what does Aether look like? He's one of the oldest gods in all of existence. Is he, like, really old?"

Hermes frowned and shook his head. "No, he appears the same age as me. And he's beautiful and handsome, which makes him all the more dangerous. He's like Apollo but a hundred times worse. He likes causing chaos for chaos's sake."

"Oh, that's terrifying."

"And with you now the queen of the underworld, I'm not quite sure what he will do."

"What do you mean?"

"I mean, he's patient. Very patient. He's been quiet, at least in the godly sphere, and it has always made me worry. He likes to stir up things for the human side of the world, of course, but that is only because he likes making humans suffer."

"I see."

After everything that had happened, I learned that while there were some gods I could trust, such as Hermes, there were plenty of others I couldn't. Everyone had an agenda and knew they would have to wait for the right moment. Gods had to be patient, and if Aether was one of the first gods in existence, perhaps he really could wait for thousands of years for whatever he had planned.

But I needed the paper translated. I needed to do this. No matter what it took.

Hermes made me wear an eye mask so I couldn't see how he got out of the underworld. Once we were on Earth, I sighed.

"Is it still really necessary you blindfold me? I'm not my father. I don't mind you coming to the underworld."

"It's a safety precaution. I don't want anyone knowing it, just in case. Remember, gods are fickle creatures."

"Whatever." I glanced around to find giant buildings surrounding me. "Whoa."

"Hong Kong is a bit more dense than the cities you visited. Keep close, there are also a lot of people."

He wasn't joking. Even in the underworld I had never seen so many people packed together. I felt crowded and stuck as the buildings felt as if they were gods themselves and I was just a little creature who didn't matter. Was this what Huntley felt like constantly? I did not like it and couldn't wait until I was back home. This was all too much for me.

And if this was too much for me, what would meeting Aether be like?

We kept walking, and I stayed close to Hermes. It was evening now, and the bright lights of all the buildings made it feel like this place never slept or never stopped running. I thought Olympus was bad, but this was much worse. I was definitely like Hades—an introvert through and through. I wanted all this to be over.

Hermes glanced down at me. "We can call it quits, and I can take you back to the underworld if you would like. You don't seem to be enjoying it here."

"I'm fine. Just take me where I need to go."

Hermes nodded and we kept moving forward. After what felt like thirty minutes of walking, we turned down a very dirty and sketchy alleyway. Of course it would be down here. At least I didn't have to worry about anything—I could protect myself with my powers, not to mention Hermes was with me.

"Second door on the right." He turned toward the way we came. "I'll be in that café over there when you are done. Remember—one hour."

I nodded and faced the door. Here went nothing.

CHAPTER TWELVE

Huntley

Hermes had left a note for me. The moment I could no longer see Chrys, I grabbed it and opened it.

She wants to talk to Aether. Thought I would let you know where we are really going. I am concerned, as you know as well as I he is not the best god to mingle with.

What would she want with Aether? I tapped my hand on the table. This made no sense—she never lied to me like this.

But was it my business to go after her? Whatever it was, she would be back quickly. At least that was what she'd said. Hermes was with her, so she couldn't get into much trouble. I would just ask her about it when she got back.

Except then I would have to tell her Hermes ratted her out. I doubted she would take that well. I let out a sigh. I really couldn't just go after her, could I? I was a human. It wasn't like any of this was my business. I needed to let her do the things she needed to cope. But what that had to do with Aether, I had no idea. From what I knew, she had never met the guy. So why would she lie to me and then go to meet with him?

My leg was shaking anxiously now. I really didn't know what to do. I didn't have anyone here I could talk to about this—nor did I have a quick way to get out of here. I was completely alone.

Like all those times growing up.

I shook my head. No, this was definitely different. I knew Chrys loved me, but there were a lot of things she was dealing with—godly things that I just didn't understand. No, I just needed to keep my cool and trust in Chrys. She wouldn't get into trouble; she wasn't stupid enough to.

Except she was stupid enough to be persuaded by AJ to visit the mortal realm even though her father forbade it. And for the past couple of weeks, she had been searching for something in Hades's study quite obsessively—even more so than normal. Did she find something?

But what could she really be looking for? Just a note from her father? But he didn't know he was going to die that day. So what could she be looking for?

For a moment I wondered if she'd found a way to release her father. But that couldn't be possible, could it? Tartarus couldn't be opened? And if it could, wouldn't that release everything?

I stood up and headed toward where Charon brought in the souls of the dead. Odds were that he wasn't there, but I could wait, as I needed him to take me to Maka. Only she would know the possibility of what I was thinking. Then she could tell me what I needed to do to keep Chrys safe.

As I arrived at the gondola port, I found that Charon was just entering the dock. I had gotten lucky for once.

"Hey, Charon," I called as I ran up to him. "Can you do me a favor?"

He nodded. "For the prince of the underworld, of course! What does Your Majesty need?"

It was still strange being called majesty. I didn't hate it, but I didn't care for it either. "Can you take me to Maka's?"

"Sure can! It's on my way back up to get souls. Hop in."

I did just that and prepared myself for the tedious ride over. Charon kept talking, but I didn't hear any of it. I just kept thinking about what mess Chrys had gotten herself into.

Charon dropped me off at Maka's, and I hurried to her door, knocking gently. "Maka, are you there?"

There was no sound. I cursed under my breath. Just my luck. I knocked a little louder.

"Maka?"

"Yes?" a voice said behind me.

I jumped and turned to find Maka standing behind me with a basket full of plants.

"What are you doing here, Huntley? I haven't had the pleasure of you visiting before. Please, come in. I'll make you some tea." She went to unlock the door.

"I just wanted to ask you why Chrys was here a few

days ago."

"Oh? And why is that?"

"She… Hermes is taking her to Aether, and I just want to make sure she is fine."

Maka stopped fiddling with the door and turned to me. "She did what?"

"What did she come here for?"

Maka let out a breath. "She is worse than her mother. She came here with a strange piece of paper that was written in primordial language. She wants to know what's on it."

"What do you think is on it?"

"Well, I thought it was a note for her from her father, but since then I started to have my doubts. If that were the case, then she would have told us the truth instead of acting weird about it."

"Maka, I'm going to ask you an important question. Is it possible to open up Tartarus?"

She didn't look me in the eye as she stepped into the house. I followed her as she set her basket down and leaned on her hands against the table.

"Do you really think Chrys would go to such lengths?"

"I think… I think she almost destroyed the world

when she was angry. She destroyed Zeus in the blink of an eye and hasn't been the same. I can't blame her, but I worry she might do something wrong."

Maka turned to me. "Then you must go to find her. She can't get that paper translated by him. It might have the information she needs to accomplish that goal. He's not a good man—in fact he's pretty terrible. He brings such horror to the world—horrors that I'll never forgive." She clutched herself tightly. "And if his children are able to leave Tartarus, I don't know what will happen to the world, not to mention the Titans. There are so many horrible things down there. I'm not sure what would happen."

"I'll do what I can, but how do I get there quickly? It's not exactly easy to leave the underworld."

"I can get you up there and will have Thanatos take over the castle, just to make sure nothing happens when you are gone."

I nodded. "Thank you. I appreciate that."

"Just give me a moment. I have to call him and settle some other stuff. Feel free to take a seat here."

I sat down on her couch and peered around. I had never visited here before, but Maka had come to the castle a few times in the past two years, so I knew her style. She was like a hippie bog witch but nicer and prettier. Her home was very, very earthy, even though we were in the underworld. From what I knew of her, she was created by Hades to help manage the souls of the blessed, so mainly the souls of those in Asphodel Meadows, which was why her home was close to that part of the underworld.

As she gathered her things and made a few calls, I wondered how we were going to reach Chrys quick enough. Hermes was the one who'd taken her, probably not knowing the truth of why she wanted to talk to Aether but suspicious enough to tell me. Did Maka have a secret way out of the underworld that I didn't know about? I mean, there was a lot I still didn't know, so it was very, very possible.

Glancing around, I wondered how many years of stuff she had collected and if this was from the underworld or if she traveled to Earth frequently. It didn't seem like she traveled to the human world all that much, as most of the underworld didn't leave often, and of course the souls couldn't. The only reason I could was because I was given the ability by Chrys.

Maka finally came back into the room. "All right, let's go."

I stood up and followed her outside, back behind the house. There was a small stream that led into a boat garage. She opened it, and I was surprised at what I saw —a gondola with an electric motor on the back.

"Whoa. You're a genius."

"I figured I could use it for emergencies. If I had known when Persephone was trying to get Chrys to the castle quickly, perhaps I could have used it. No matter. Hermes would have eventually found her anyway."

I thought back to that time, and it was true—Hermes, once he'd known Chrys was here, would have stopped at nothing for Zeus because of his fear of him. But he had helped a lot, so I couldn't exactly be mad at him.

"Now get on. We are going for a fun ride."

CHAPTER THIRTEEN

Chrys

I wasn't sure what I expected, but as I stepped inside, I felt both shock and fear engulf my senses. Humans filled the front area, most lying on blankets and pillows, intoxicated with some kind of smoked herb. I held my hand to my mouth as the smell of burned sugar and licorice filled the air. What was this? Was this a drug?

By the looks of everyone around, it had to be. Some people didn't appear to be moving. My eyes widened as I watched their souls weakening.

Was this what Aether was up to? Was he really causing all this despair and darkness?

"Hello, little lady, are you lost?" a human said in Mandarin as he stumbled up and started walking toward me.

I didn't know what to do or say but just stared at him.

He came closer. "How about you hang here with me? I'll pay for your first round."

The man tried to reach for me, but I grabbed his wrist and started to squeeze it. I heard bones crack as he screamed out.

"Please let my patron go. I try to keep a pretty relaxed atmosphere, if you can't tell."

I turned to find a man with long white hair that gently draped over his shoulders. He wore a black robe that had a golden dragon embroidered into it. He had an air about him that was almost irresistible—as if you were intrigued and yet knew not to trust anything he said or did. I wanted to learn more, and yet at the same time, I wanted to run back to Hermes to take me home.

No, I had a mission—I had to do this. I would do anything to save my father.

I let the man go, and he collapsed on the ground. A couple of women dressed in short dresses carried him to one of the blankets and helped him with his next smoke. I gulped, not sure what this drug was doing to all of them, but it didn't appear to be good.

The god in front of me took a whiff of his own long pipe and blew the smoke slowly. "So, what does the queen of the underworld want from me?"

I glanced around, confused as to why he would be so upfront about being a god with all these humans. Then I realized they were barely coherent and probably didn't even notice.

"I need a favor from you. Is there a place we could talk alone?"

He nodded. "Yes, follow me."

I followed him into the back of the business he had running. As we traveled from room to room, I saw that he didn't only sell to humans but to gods and all sorts of creatures as well. I saw sirens, nymphs, satyrs, and even an empusa. I tried not to stare at them all, as I didn't come across any of their kind that often in the underworld. They lived long lives, and there weren't many compared to humans.

As we kept on traveling, I realized that Aether was one of the only gods who was well known by everyone except me. Why was that? Why didn't my father teach me about this god when he'd taught me about everything else? Was it because he held the secret to opening Tartarus?

We made it to the back room where a few girls were lying around a large couch. They all appeared high like the other patrons and were wearing the same short, tight dresses that the women who were serving the drug were. This must have been the break room, or these were the women who served only Aether.

"Leave us," Aether commanded with a soft voice.

All the women got up and dragged themselves out of the room without question. Aether took a seat and patted the space next to him.

"Have a seat."

I shook my head. "Nah, I'm good standing."

"Suit yourself." He leaned back and crossed his legs. "Now, tell me, why is the queen of the underworld in my humble abode?"

I hesitated. Why was I so scared of him? I could

easily end him if I wanted—there was no need to be afraid. I had defeated Zeus with my power. There was no way I could be hurt by this god.

And yet here I stood, shaking. Was it the smoke in the air making me feel like this? Or was it something else? Did my instinct know that he was a god before gods existed? Why was I so afraid?

"I'm waiting." Aether took another puff, and the sweet, sugary scent surrounded him.

I took a deep breath. "I found a paper that contains primordial writing in my father's study. I want to know what's on it."

He raised an eyebrow. "Oh? Let me see it."

I pulled it out of my pocket and handed it to him. I was afraid that he might destroy it, but I had made a copy I had hidden away. If he tried to stop me, I could still find someone else to translate it. Eventually.

He read through it with a smile on his lips. He appeared as if he were calculating something before he peered back up at me.

"Tell me this, what do you think is on this piece of paper?"

I froze. If I was right, it was a way to open up Tartarus, but what if I was wrong? What if it was something completely different and I would be admitting to him what my intentions were? Would he tell on me? Was coming here a big mistake?

"I… I don't know. I was just curious, that's all."

He let out a laugh that shook me to my core. "You honestly think I would believe that?" He took a puff of his pipe as he studied me. "Gods of the underworld don't just leave their post on a whim. There has to be an important reason for them to leave. You believe something is on this paper, and I want to know what you came all the way down here for."

I bit my lip. Should I tell him? Would anyone believe him if I spoke the truth? Would he do as I asked if I told him?

"I… I think it's a way to get my father back." It was vague enough that it could mean anything.

He giggled a little. "I see." He stood up and stepped in front of me. Although I had noticed earlier, he was tall. I stared up at him, but my eyes only went to his chest. He peered down at me and blew smoke right into my face.

"And how do you expect to save your father, hmm? Three clicks of some ruby shoes? Find a fairy godmother?"

I shook my head. "I don't know."

He held up the note. "But you believe it's on this piece of paper."

I frowned. "You already know, otherwise you wouldn't be asking me all this."

He placed his finger under my chin and stroked my cheek with his thumb. "What are you willing to do for this information?"

I narrowed my eyes but didn't say anything because, honestly, I was willing to do anything. But if I found out the paper did not, in fact, have a way to help my father, then I would kill him. It was as simple as that.

"What do you want?"

His eyes glanced down at my lips. I felt my heart quicken. He let go of my chin and went back to his sofa.

"I'm actually more interested in that husband of yours."

"What? What would you want with Huntley? How do you even know him?"

He took a whiff of his pipe. "He came here when you were kidnapped and at Circe's. I found him to be quite interesting and want to talk to him some more."

I didn't like where this was going. It was clear that

Aether wanted to cause trouble, and with Huntley's history as a human, I couldn't imagine him coming in here. Even in the underworld he found the pomegranates to get high on. I had a feeling if he came here again, he would never be able to leave even if I was here.

"I will not bring you to him."

Aether's eyes widened. "Really? You care more about him than your own father?"

I shook my head. "What I feel for Huntley is different than my father. They aren't comparable. His life isn't for me to give."

"I don't want his life. I want him just to try a taste of this." He lifted the pipe. "It's nothing he can't handle."

"If he knows of this place and hasn't come on his own, then I know he is trying to stay away from you. I will not subject him to such torture."

He chuckled. "Fine. Then how about you try it?"

I frowned. "I've never—"

"Don't lie to me. You have had those pomegranates. This is much less drastic than those." He patted the space next to him. "Now, come sit next to me."

I didn't want to, but I had to do whatever I could to keep Huntley safe and to save my father. I sat down next to him, keeping my distance from his body. That didn't matter as he placed his arm behind me and leaned into me, handing me his pipe.

"One puff, that's all I ask of you," he whispered in my ear.

What could the harm be in just breathing in once? I took the pipe and placed it on my lips.

CHAPTER FOURTEEN

Huntley

Man, the motorboat went a lot faster than the gondola I was used to. I honestly thought I was going to fall off the back if I didn't hold on, like all those sketchy fairground rides when I was a kid. I was surprised there weren't more accidents at fairgrounds because of those.

We passed by Charon, who waved at us even though I was pretty sure we weren't supposed to be driving with anything so fast. I tried to wave back but was too afraid to let go. What would happen if I fell out? Would I fall into the water to be floating for decades? Or would I miss the water and fall down into nothingness? I didn't want to find out the answer to that the hard way.

But I had to admit, this was a nicer way to travel in the underworld. Everything, other than Hermes, was so much slower. I guess in death, there really was no need to hurry.

The gate to Earth was coming up, and I shut my eyes as I swore we were going to run right into it. Suddenly we stopped, and I held on with all my might, and after a few seconds opened my eyes. Maka was smiling at me.

"Really, Huntley? Did my driving frighten you that much?"

I didn't say a word as we got out of the boat and walked through the portal. I had to admit, going through the gate was a lot nicer than straight through Oceanus as we had when Chrys, AJ, and I snuck out that one time. Apparently that was not the standard way to get out. That definitely made sense.

"So, is he still in Hong Kong?" I asked as we started off. It was clear we were somewhere that used Chinese symbols, but other than that, I had no idea. It wasn't like I had come here often.

"Yes. He still has that opium den. It's fascinating he hasn't been caught, or perhaps he paid all the cops off. Usually he moved around, but he's stayed in this location for quite some time."

I nodded. "Right."

Maka glanced at me. "Are you all right?"

I shrugged. "No? I mean, my wife was lying to me, and while I understand that, I still don't feel good about it. I want to support her, but she isn't giving me much to work with. Then to top it off, she goes to Aether, who is like some drug lord. Is she okay? Am I going to be able to help her? I mean, last time I was there, I had the will to get out of there because I had to go save her, but now..." I shook my head. "I don't know if I would be able to leave."

"Ah. There's no shame in admitting that, Huntley. Plenty of gods have the same problem. Having that moment of relief is intoxicating, and when that is the only way to feel good, it becomes addicting. But you will have me there, so don't worry. I'll keep you safe from Aether."

I smiled. "Thanks. You are pretty cool, you know that?"

"I do! I'm one of the best."

I laughed as we headed farther down the streets. I was glad Maka was with me as I wouldn't have any idea where I was going. It had been a while, and we didn't go too far through the city.

The farther we walked, the sketchier everything started to appear. It was apparent we were getting closer. Each city had a dark area, and if I knew anything from growing up, that was exactly where to find a dealer. I took a deep breath to calm myself down. I was past this—I didn't have to worry any longer. I had friends who cared about me and a wife who was dear to me. I couldn't fall into that all again.

And what would even happen if I did? Technically I was dead, so it wasn't like I ran that risk. Perhaps it wouldn't be really that bad if I did do anything. Did that settle my nerves? No. Did I think that actually made it worse? Perhaps.

Maka stopped in front of an alleyway. "Okay, his place is down this way. Are you ready to do this?"

Before I could answer, I heard a voice behind me.

"Huntley? Maka? Is that you guys?"

Both of us turned to find Hermes hurrying toward us.

"Oh, it is! That was fast. Actually, I didn't think you would come all the way here. I just figured you would talk to her when she got back."

"How long has she been in there?" Maka asked.

Hermes checked his watch. "Half an hour. I told her I would go in after her if she was in there for more than an hour."

I glanced back down the alleyway. "Then what should we do? Should we go in now or should we wait?"

Hermes shrugged. "I really don't know. If we go in, Aether might try something. But if we leave Chrys to what she is doing…" He peered at us to see if we knew what was up.

I shook my head. "We aren't sure, but I have a feeling it has something to do with Tartarus. Otherwise, she would have told us all."

Hermes nodded. "Yeah, that was what I was thinking, which is why I left that note. If she finds out, she's probably going to kill me."

"Which brings us back to the question of what should we do?"

Maka bit her thumb. "I really don't know. I understand r wanting to find a way to bring back Hades, but she knows what she's doing is wrong."

"Is it though?" I asked.

Hermes and Maka both answered at the same time. "Yes."

Hermes sighed. "Look, I know you also cared for Hades, and none of us thinks he deserved to go to Tartarus, but there is no way we can do anything to help him at this point. I was only able to save you and Chrys because I acted fast and you weren't in deep, not to mention Kronos doesn't have a grudge against you."

I raised an eyebrow. "What do you mean, Chrys?"

Both Maka and I started at him. Hermes fidgeted. "Yeah, so, when I was down there and watching Chrys for Zeus, she fell into Tartarus. Luckily I witnessed it and dove down to save her. She freaked out, and I almost lost my life right then and there."

Maka shook her head. "That's not possible— someone can't just fall into Tartarus. They have to be sent there."

Hermes shrugged. "I don't know what to tell you. I saw what I saw. But she's fine, so I wouldn't worry about it. She claimed something grabbed her, but that can't be possible. It was weird, but it never happened again."

I wasn't sure why this was the first time I was hearing this. A lot had happened since then—Prometheus kidnapping her and erasing her memories and all that. I would have assumed that it would have come up in conversation in the past two years—especially since I was sent to Tartarus as well.

But that wasn't the point right now. Right now we needed to do something about Aether and whatever Chrys was doing. I couldn't exactly go in as the place was too tempting and I wasn't sure what would happen if I smoked that drug that was in there. No, other than the pomegranates, I gave up that life. I had to keep moving forward.

Hermes checked his watch. "I say we all wait for her. She has thirty minutes left, and we watch her reaction when she gets out and then interrogate her with the information we know. Does that sound like a plan?"

Maka and I nodded, as I doubted she wanted to go in there either.

"Is it all right if I go wander around? I don't like sitting still."

Hermes laughed and nodded. "Yes, but don't venture

far. I don't want to have to try to find you in this place."

I nodded. "I won't. Be back here before the half hour is over."

Turning, I left them to stay at the café. I made a note of where they were and tried not to travel too far—I just wanted to move around.

How much was Chrys keeping from me? Should I be worried? I understood her frustration, but it was beginning to scare me.

I turned around a corner. I decided it would be easiest just to round a block, as I wouldn't get lost if I went in a complete circle.

This place felt so busy, but that made me feel utterly alone. Should I really be here? Did I really have any authority to stop Chrys? She was just trying to help her father. It had been two years since he was sent to Tartarus, and I hadn't seen her smile like she used to. Wouldn't this be for the better? Wouldn't anyone else do the same thing to save their loved one from eternal torment?

No one seemed to be trying to save Zeus or Poseidon, or at least not to my knowledge. It didn't seem like that many were sad or surprised by their passing at the funeral for the three gods. Hades, however, had the entire underworld in tears. He was loved by any who actually knew him, which was not the same for the others.

I took a deep breath. Why couldn't this be easy? Why couldn't there be a way to save Hades since Chrys was the queen of the underworld? It should be simple to retrieve someone from Tartarus if need be, but it wasn't.

As I was about to round another corner, I felt as if I were being watched. I stopped and turned but didn't notice anyone suspicious. Perhaps it was my imagination as I wasn't used to being around so many people, and Zeus sent people after me so many times when I was in London.

I started walking again when suddenly I felt something go over my head and I was pulled off the street.

CHAPTER FIFTEEN

Chrys

What was wrong with me?

I only took in one puff, and I felt as if everything around me had shifted. It was similar to the pomegranates, but I had more control when I ate those. If anything, it felt as if I had eaten a dozen of them. I felt happy, and everything around me seemed pleasant. I wanted more, but deep down I knew that was wrong.

But was it? I tried to decide if there was really any

reason for me to not want another puff of that drug. I was a god; it couldn't really hurt me. I wasn't a human who would become addicted or have any physical problems from it, so there was no reason to keep enjoying this a little longer.

I reached out to Aether's hand, bringing the pipe to my lips once again. He grinned devilishly and chuckled.

"That's right, Chrys, let everything go and indulge. This is what we gods deserve to do. We are to be served while we are enjoying such euphoric experiences."

I couldn't disagree with that. I breathed in the lovely scent and slowly breathed out, watching the smoke leave my mouth. Aether took another puff himself, and I leaned back in the chair, staring up at the ceiling.

If I could, I would stay like that forever. Everything felt nice—it was a sensation that I hadn't experienced in such a long time. Why did so many think that this was wrong when it felt so good? My entire body relaxed, and I thought for a moment I would simply melt into the couch I found myself on.

Aether turned to me, his finger gently intertwining with my hair. Now that I wasn't afraid, I had to admit, he was quite handsome in a certain way. He had that strong, chiseled face that so many found attractive. He was dirty in a just-worked-out sort of way. His long white hair shimmered in the light, and if I wasn't wrong, his eyes were the color of the night sky with sparkles just like the stars. It was no wonder so many followed him in his dark ways. He was just that beautiful.

"You know, goddess of the underworld, I never imagined someone so beautiful like you could exist."

I could feel my face warm, even though it was already warm from whatever was in the pipe. I turned away. "Oh no, those girls who were in here were a lot more attractive than I am."

He took a strand of my hair and gently kissed it with his lips. "No, you are a lot more beautiful. It is no wonder Zeus tried to keep you for himself."

I didn't quite understand what was going on. Everything was a blur. Zeus? Oh right, he tried to marry me. It was a bother, but it didn't matter any longer. I was here, and I was happy.

"Your mother is one of the most beautiful women in all the lands. But don't tell Aphrodite or Hera I said such things. They might kill me even though I am quite stronger than them. But it seems you inherited her looks and are even more lovely than she is."

I didn't like being compared to my mother, but I had to admit, she was beautiful. I never imagined myself looking better than her.

Shaking my head, I fiddled with my fingers. Something felt odd, as if I was forgetting something. What was it?

"No, I'm nothing like her. You flatter me too much."

He gently turned my chin to face him. "No, I don't flatter you enough."

Aether leaned in and kissed my lips. He tasted of burned sugar and licorice, just like the drug did. And like the drug, I wanted more. I grabbed him by the hem of his robe and pulled him closer. His kiss deepened, and I felt his tongue against my teeth.

I wanted this, right? Then why did something feel off? I wanted to indulge in this euphoric feeling, but something was wrong. Why was I here? Had I always been here? Or was there something else going on that I was forgetting?

At that moment, it didn't matter. I wanted this feeling to last forever, and the more I kissed Aether, the more I kept feeling it. It was as if he were one with the drug, and the more of him I tasted, the more of the feeling I drank. I would be happy if this lasted forever, no matter what the consequence was.

I pulled him down against the couch. He was heavy on top of me, but it was warming all the same. His kisses were harder, and I felt as if I could melt into him.

The more we were there, the more a strange feeling came over me. It wasn't as nice as the rest of what I was feeling, so I kept trying to push it back, but there was something bothering me. Why did something about this feel familiar but not? It was as if he should have been someone else, but he wasn't.

I didn't like this feeling. I wanted it to go away—I wanted to just be happy. I wanted to be free.

"Chrys, snap out of it."

It was a voice that came from nowhere. It sounded familiar—it sounded like…

I screamed as I used my power of darkness and unleashed it throughout the room. I know one of the tendrils smacked into Aether, and he flew back a bit. A black web spread across his chest and up to his throat. He peered down at the mark with marvel.

"So it is true. I mean, I assumed it was if you sent Zeus and Poseidon to Tartarus, but I wanted to see it for myself."

"You bastard! What did you do to me?" I yelled.

Aether grabbed his pipe. "Nothing anyone has ever been able to shake off. You are one powerful goddess, I'll give you that." He took a puff as he glanced behind himself. "But it seems I have gotten what I wanted in the end, so I'll translate this paper for you."

My eyes widened. That was right—I was here to get something translated. Whatever he gave me was strong enough to even cause me to forget that. I didn't like this place anymore, not that I liked it in the beginning. I understood why Hermes didn't want to come in and why everyone warned me. But I had been able to snap out of it and knocked him around pretty well.

Then it hit me—whose voice was that? It sounded like someone impossible. It had sounded like my father, but he couldn't have done that from Tartarus. Could he have?

I shook my head. It was an illusion, probably my own mind getting the attention it needed to bring me back to reality. I watched Aether as he set his pipe down and grabbed a pen.

"Will English do?" he asked as he started scribbling.

I nodded. "That's fine. That's what Huntley speaks, so we typically use that."

"Such an interesting boy, that one. He has such

cravings, you know that? I bet he would lose himself in a place like this."

"You can't have him."

Aether grinned. "Whatever you say." He finished writing and handed me the paper. "Now tell me what you think of that."

I examined the paper. It read "With the twin torches of Hekate, one may destroy the gate of Tartarus." That was it.

"Is it really that simple?" I asked.

Aether laughed. "You think taking Hekate's torches is simple? She is one of the scariest goddesses in all of existence. Even with your powers I'm not sure you could sneak in and defeat her. Not many know the power of those torches—even I didn't know Tartarus could be opened with them. I have a feeling only she and Hades knew, and there is a reason for that."

"Because it will release everything?"

Aether nodded. "Are you willing to risk that for your father?"

"I am. And I'm sure I can put everything back after I get my father out of there."

"Oh, you are a brave one, aren't you?"

I glanced back at the paper. Was it really that simple?

"And what about you? Why would you willingly tell me how to open the gates when you know it's possible I may succeed?"

He grinned. "I look forward to seeing my children once more. You aren't the only one who has lost someone to that pit." He took a breath of his pipe. "So many have been wrongfully placed there. It was a matter of time before someone snapped and went to release them."

"Well, I'm glad to be of service. Is there anything else you wish to give me on this quest?"

Aether stepped forward and twirled his finger around my hair. I glared at him. "I hope you succeed and don't die. I rather like you."

I swatted his hand away. "Then I thank you for your help. And I hope we will never cross paths again."

He laughed as I turned and left the facility. I wasn't lying. I didn't know what I would do if I was offered that pipe once more.

CHAPTER SIXTEEN

Huntley

I didn't know what was happening. Everything had gone dark, and no matter how much I tried to fight, whoever had me was a lot stronger. I had a feeling it had to be a god, but who in the world was targeting me now? People mad about Chrys killing Zeus and Poseidon? Or someone else?

They quickly bound my arms behind my back, and two of them guided me down an alleyway of some sort, or I presumed it was a creepy, dark, alleyway as there was no way this would have not been suspicious on the street. Then again, this was a dark and shady part of Hong Kong.

"Where are you taking me? Who are you?" I yelled. Suddenly the two people stopped and I felt a knee to my stomach.

"Shut up! Be quiet!"

I wanted to bend over in pain, but the two kept me up. "You could have just said that," I wheezed out.

The two assailants led me farther, and I pondered what I should do. They were definitely stronger, something I learned to assess when I was young and got into fights quite often. I also was curious where I was being led since it was clear whoever was kidnapping me wanted me specifically. Curiosity always got the better of me.

As for my hands, I held them in a certain way that would be somewhat easier to get out of. By the feeling on my skin, it was clear they had used a zip tie, but I had moved my hands and wrists so that it left a gap. I would definitely have to either use my shoestring to cut it or dislocate something. It all depended on the situation I would find myself in.

Suddenly I was shoved through a door and I heard it close behind me. There were voices and some music, but that wasn't the most telling thing about the room. No, I knew exactly where I was now and who had captured me after I smelled the sweet nectar of opium.

It was Aether. He had for some reason captured me.

But why? How did he even know I was near? Did he figure since Chrys was talking to him that I wouldn't be far away? I supposed it was true, so I couldn't blame him for thinking that. But what would he want me for? It wasn't like I was that important.

Then again, Maka had said he just liked causing problems for chaos's sake. Perhaps he wanted something from Chrys and I would be the only way to get to her. That was the only conclusion I could come up with.

I was pushed through the building for a while. I couldn't make out any single voice, and most were in some kind of Asian language, although I didn't know which it was since I knew nothing about those languages. I knew there were big differences, but to my ear, I had no reference to go off of. The gods, however, could speak all of them, and perhaps someday I could as well.

Suddenly we stopped and I was forced to my knees. There was no other noise in this room, and I presumed I was to wait here for Aether or whatever god was here if it wasn't in fact him that summoned me. I still wasn't sure of his motive, but I knew I would soon find out.

The air was still stagnant with the smoke, and with every moment that passed, the more my skin began to itch and my heart rate quickened. I was both cold and hot, as if I had a fever. I didn't want to breathe any of it in, but I couldn't help it—it was all around me, and I still had to breathe. I had to fight the urges—I had to make sure I didn't fall down that hole again even if I was already dead.

Because I knew once I started, I would never want to leave.

I prayed that Hermes or Maka saw what happened and would come for me before it was too late. I wanted to laugh a little. Never in my life did I believe someone would rescue me when I was in situations like this. Granted, I hadn't been in this exact situation, but I had been beaten up, tied up, on drugs, and all of that without the thought of someone saving me. This hadn't been my choice like those had been, however, as this was definitely because of something bigger. But the fact still remained—I had friends who had my back now. I didn't have a reason to be afraid.

Even though I was dead, my body still definitely wanted those drugs.

The door behind me opened, but I still had a bag over my head so I couldn't see who it was. I had an idea, however.

"Well, well. Look what little rat was sniffing around my establishment," a voice said. It was smooth and definitely Aether.

"I wasn't looking for you if that is what you thought. I was looking for my wife."

"Ah, I see."

It was quiet for a moment. I thought maybe he would say something about her but apparently not.

"So, um, where is she? What have you done with her?"

"Nothing. She asked me to translate something, and I did just that, and she went on her way. You just missed her, actually."

That made no sense. Then what did he want with me? Why was I even here? "Oh. Well then, perhaps you could take this bag off of me and untie me and I'll be on my way…"

Aether laughed. "I don't think so."

So he did want me for some odd reason. "And why not?"

"Because, Huntley, we are going to have so much fun together."

I did not like the sound of that. I wanted to run and hide from this god. He was dangerous, as were most of them, but for some reason this one was focused on me. I had to figure out a way out of there.

"Well," I began. "It would be a lot funnier if I didn't have a bag over my head and my wrists bound by zip ties."

The bag came off my head, and Aether stood in front of me with his pipe. How could he smoke so much? I supposed it was because he was a god, but still. He needed to take a break. He didn't move to unbind my hands, but at least I could see now.

It was a different room than when I was here with Pothos. No, this was like a private room with some cushions and blankets scattered around. There was only a door behind me with two men guarding it. I gulped, doubting I could get past them in this state.

I turned back to my captor and smiled. "So, I would really like to leave."

He shook his head. "No, Huntley, I don't think you do. I think you want to stay here." Aether bent down and blew smoke into my face. "And have a smoke with me."

I mean, I did. I really, really did. But I couldn't let him know that. "Not particularly. I have some pomegranates waiting for me at home, and I don't want those to spoil, so I'll be getting out of your hair..." I tried to stand up, but he shoved me back down.

"Not so fast. I've seen your kind before, Huntley. You were that kid who didn't get along with anyone, weren't you? Everyone was putting you down, and all you wanted was love. So when someone handed you a smoke or a needle, you didn't even hesitate to say no, did you? Because it was the one thing that would always be there, waiting for you. It was a constant in your terrible world."

He had me pegged. I knew I wasn't the only one who had a past such as that, but I didn't like that he could tell.

"That was before. Now I'm happily married and good with my life. I have friends who will come looking for me, and I know I have somewhere to go back to."

"Is that so?"

"Yup."

Aether laughed. "I love your spunk, you know that? Kids like you are always the most fun to play with. You think you are strong, but you are oh so weak. I would like to see you fight your urges, Huntley." He took a seat on the ground and leaned back on a pillow. "How long will it take for you to bet me for a puff of this?"

I shook my head. "No, I don't want it. I am good with my life. I don't need that stuff."

"It doesn't matter if you need it. There are plenty of people happy with their life who still turn to drugs. After one taste, it is hard to turn back. It's like getting a taste of the gods, wouldn't you say? We gods get to experience this euphoric feeling for an eternity."

"But humans don't get to. No, one hit can make us weak and destroy our bodies."

"Such a dilemma for you humans then. To feel good and yet not be. I would hate to be human." He took another smoke. "But you aren't human, are you, Huntley? Not anymore. You are something that can have as much of this drug as you want and not face the consequences. You could live off of it all day and night and not have a worry."

Well, when he put it that way, I wanted to stay. But I knew that was wrong. I needed to get out of there. The problem was, I knew there was no way he was going to let me go this time. It would take a while for Hermes and Maka to come and find me, not to mention I had no idea where Chrys was now.

Then an idea hit me. "I'll try your pipe, if you tell me why my wife was here."

CHAPTER

SEVENTEEN

Chrys

Hermes was waiting for me when I stepped outside. He appeared worried, more than likely because we were approaching the one-hour mark. He saw me coming over and began to speak when I stopped him.

"Sorry I took so long, and thank you for bringing me up here, but I am going to head back on my own from here."

He glanced around. "Oh, you are?"

I nodded. "Yeah, I have some things to think about after reading my father's note to me. I'd rather ponder them alone, if that's all right."

Hermes seemed as if he was trying to figure out how to stop me or something else. I really didn't want him to come along as I needed to go to Hekate's instead of my castle. Huntley would notice me back and would find it suspicious if I went away again. I needed to go straight from the entrance of the underworld to head to Hekate's. It was deep in the underworld—as deep as one could get. She liked to keep to herself except that time when she helped Demeter screw over my parents' relationship. I still had no idea why she did that, and I decided when I heard that story that I wouldn't want to speak to her ever. So I'd stayed away from her house until today.

"Fine. Yeah, I need to help someone with something anyway. Just promise me you will go straight home."

I nodded. "Of course."

He stared at me for a moment, then held out his hand.

"Pinky swear."

I laughed, then took his pinky swear. "I swear I'll go straight to the underworld."

"All right then. I'll see you later, Chrys."

"See you."

He hurried off in a different direction. I was surprised he let me off the hook that easily. He must have really been distracted by something. Well, now he could take care of whatever it was and not have to worry about me.

I strode off in the opposite direction, looking for a space where I could teleport to the entrance of the underworld. Before she disappeared from my life, my mother taught me how to teleport on Earth if the occasion ever arose. I wish we could teleport like that in the underworld, but it seemed that my father made that impossible. It made sense, as there shouldn't be anyone in the underworld that would need to or else they could cause problems. Like Hermes used to.

Glancing up, I was still very impressed and a little frightened how amazing this city was. It was so bright and busy. I knew there would be no way I could live here. I liked the quiet parts about the underworld and the darkness that it possessed. This place had way too much going on—too much for a girl like me.

Rounding a quiet corner, I snapped my fingers. In an instant, I found myself in front of the gates of the underworld. I would have to wait for Charon to come for his next batch of souls. By the looks of it, it wouldn't be too long since there were quite a bit of souls lining up.

I made my way to the front of the line. "Excuse me, pardon me, queen of the underworld coming through."

They all moved for me, both confused and flabbergasted that I was in fact the queen of the afterlife for them. These souls were all ones that needed to be judged. It appeared my work was already piling up. It was no matter, however, as after I would do what I was about to do, these souls would probably be set free. I apparently couldn't change that fact.

Now that I thought about it, how many souls were down there? Would human souls be set free? Would they go back to the mortal realm, or would they just kind of be stuck in the underworld roaming around? That would be a lot of cleanup. But once my father was let out, I could close the door and hope that most of the human souls wouldn't be set free. It would be fine.

Right?

My stomach began to knot. Did I really know what

was going to happen, or was I just hoping for the best? If it was possible to open the gates of Tartarus, that meant that it wouldn't be that catastrophic, right? I couldn't imagine it would destroy everything. No, it would be okay. I would get my father, then he and I would close the gate and take care of whatever escaped. Easy peasy.

At least that was what I hoped.

I could still turn back at this point, I knew. The only other person who knew what I wanted to do was Aether, and I doubted he would have a way to open the gates. He even admitted getting the torches from Hekate would be difficult, and he didn't want anything to do with her. So perhaps I could just go home, have a nice evening with Huntley, and forget everything that happened today.

But then my father would still be in Tartarus, suffering for the mistake I had made.

I clenched my hand. No, I couldn't let him keep suffering. I had to do something.

So to Hekate's it was, once Charon showed up, of course. These human souls would have to wait until Charon took me where I needed to go and came back. It wasn't like they didn't have eternity anyway.

While I waited, I wondered what I would tell Charon. It wasn't like I could tell him the truth, of course, and I had no idea what sort of excuse I would need to give, not that I needed to give an excuse. I more just needed to tell him something so he would stop pestering me.

I hadn't ever met her, so perhaps I could say since I was the queen of the underworld, I wanted to go introduce myself. Yeah, that made sense. It was decided.

About forty minutes passed when Charon finally arrived. He was singing *(Don't Fear) the Reaper* by Blue Öyster Cult as the doors opened and he came into view. Everyone was staring at him, afraid, but I simply rolled my eyes. Was this really how he treated the recently departed? I might have to talk to him later. Then again, these were souls I needed to judge. I couldn't blame him for having a little fun with it. I guess I would let this slide.

As he got closer, he squinted and waved his hand. "Your Majesty! I didn't realize you had left! What brought you to the mortal realm?"

"I had some business with Hermes. But I need you to take me to Hekate before you take some souls to the castle. Can you do that?" I asked as I stepped up to the dock.

He nodded. "For the queen of the underworld, I can do anything." Charon turned to the rest of the souls waiting. "Bow down to your queen! She is the one ruling the underworld!"

I did not want to deal with this right now. I turned to find all the humans either very, very confused or doing as he said and bowing. I smiled to them and turned to Charon.

"Let's just get out of here," I commented as I got on the boat.

"As you wish, Your Majesty."

He began paddling and we were off. We went a whole minute before Charon began talking.

"So, why do you want to see Hekate? You have never visited her before."

Just as I suspected. I sighed. "Oh, you know, I'm the queen of the underworld now, so I figured I would get to know everyone down here."

"That makes sense. We already know each other pretty well, so I guess you won't need to visit me, now will you."

I pinched the bridge of my nose. "Nope, I won't need to."

"Well, Hekate is an interesting woman. She's super old, even older than me. She was the one who helped Demeter find your mother all those years ago. I always wondered if she hadn't helped Demeter, whether Persephone would have stayed in the underworld all the time instead of just three months of the year. I guess we will never know, will we?"

"Nope, guess not."

I really did blame Hekate for half my problems. If she hadn't caused issues for my parents, then my mom wouldn't have turned out to be a bitch, and I wouldn't have gone to the mortal realm. Then my father wouldn't be in Tartarus.

I sighed as we kept traveling. Charon was talking about something, but I wasn't paying attention anymore. After all these years, I had gotten pretty good at tuning him out when I had other things on my mind. I glanced around, wondering how long it would take us, and how much would change once I opened the gates to Tartarus. Would I be able to make it all go back to normal? I had to be able to or else how would I live with myself? But my father was powerful, just like I was. He and I could put the rest of the souls back.

There was also the matter of Zeus. I would get to that

when I got to it though. First thing was first—I had to steal the two torches from Hekate.

We traveled for an hour when finally we arrived at Hekate's place. It was large. Not as large as my castle, but it was a lot bigger than I expected. This worked to my advantage, however, as then I could sneak around and get in with the less likely chance she would notice. I would just have to figure out where exactly the two torches were.

As we paddled in, I realized I would need a boat back. Shit. I turned to Charon.

"Is it possible for you to make me a boat that I could get back home with?"

He nodded and snapped his fingers. Another boat appeared behind us. "How else do you think I am able to cart so many souls at a time?"

That was fair. I supposed he did need more boats as soon as possible.

"Thank you."

"Do you know the way back?"

I nodded. "Yeah, I'll be able to figure it out."

"Well, then I'll leave you and the boat at that dock, and you can have your fun date with Hekate."

CHAPTER EIGHTEEN

Huntley

Aether studied me as he smoked his pipe. He apparently was surprised I would pry into what information he gave Chrys or that I would make a trade such as this. After a moment, he started laughing.

"You and Chrys are quite similar. She traded information for a taste of my pipe."

My eyes widened. "She did what?"

"It was hard for her to resist. I think if she was just a little weaker, I could have gotten her to stay here forever. But alas, she snapped out of it for some reason. I wish I knew what that reason was as then I would have gone about it all differently. It is no matter. I still get something I want out of the deal."

"And that is?"

"Her opening Tartarus. Or at least trying to. I don't know how successful she will be, although now I know what to do if I ever needed to. Or I can get someone to pay me a hefty price for that knowledge. I'm just waiting to see how it all goes down."

I couldn't believe what he was saying. Chrys was going to try to open the gates of Tartarus? That didn't seem possible. Why would she do that? No, I knew the reason—she wanted to save her father. But this wasn't the way. This would release so much darkness in the world. I didn't think she really would want to risk all that just to see her father again. That would mean Zeus and Poseidon would be set free and they would try even harder to take her down.

It just didn't make sense.

Then again, I doubt she was thinking straight because of all the grief she was facing. I took a deep breath and let it out slowly. I didn't know what I was going to do about this. I had to help her. But first I needed to get out of there.

The problem was, now that he'd told me the truth, I would have to uphold my end of the bargain. Would I be able to snap out of the feeling of tranquility that I knew that pipe would give me? I know, as a human, I wouldn't be able to. But as he pointed out, I was no longer human. Perhaps I was stronger than that drug.

Or I could get up and try to make a run for it. Either way, I would have to face some sort of consequence.

Before Aether could react to what I was thinking, I bolted toward the door I prayed wasn't locked or at least was slightly ajar. The two guards tried to stop me, but I plowed my head straight into one of their stomachs. The man bent over, trying to catch his breath. The uninjured guard took a swing for me, but I ducked and swept underneath his feet. The guard fell. I turned around to try to open the door with my bound hands. Just as I got it to open and turned to run out, something grabbed me by the back of my shirt and lifted me up.

"Did you really think that would work?" Aether said in my ear. "That you would be able to escape a god?"

I shrugged. "I mean, yeah."

He laughed. "You have spunk. I like that about you. It makes me want to keep you here even more. I want to see how long it takes your wife to detect you are gone. She's so preoccupied with her father I doubt she will notice before she opens the gates of Tartarus. Then, after that, you won't even matter to her since she will have a lot to clean up."

I was trying to kick myself free, but it was no use. "Why do you even want the gates to Tartarus open? I mean, if it is just going to destroy everything, what do you stand to gain?"

"Chaos, of course. I live for it. And my children are all locked up in there. I would like to see them free and ruling the world. I am sick of those humans and what mischief they get into on their own. They need to pay for all the things that they have done in the past few centuries—they need to learn to fear us gods once more."

"Ah, so you just want power."

"Something like that."

He moved us toward the center of the room and

threw me to the ground. I hit the pillow with my face as my hands were still bound behind my back. He took another puff and blew it down to me.

"Now, you need to hold up your end of the bargain, my dear Huntley." He pulled me around so that I could face him. He placed the pipe against my mouth. I tried to back my head away, but he grabbed my jaw with his free hand.

"You have to breathe sometime. Come on, just one taste and you will be forever free. Think about it—no side effects now that you are dead. You can enjoy it forever."

I knew there was no use resisting any longer. I took a breath, and the sweet taste of opium filled my mouth. It was like black licorice mixed with burned sugar. I instantly felt it—that euphoric instinct that made me desire more. I wanted to be lost here—I wanted all the pain to simply go away. Nothing else mattered—there was no more worry. All that mattered was feeling like this and escaping.

Part of my mind screamed as I relaxed and fell back on the pillows. The screaming sounded as if I had something to live for—something that was telling me to get up and run, but I couldn't make it out. It was as if it were screaming from another room and I couldn't do anything to understand it better. Did something not here even matter? Did those words even matter? I should just keep lying here and enjoying this feeling. Nothing else mattered.

But something did matter. What was it? I felt like I should know. I felt like I had been here before, but this time was different. This time I didn't have a reason not to go home. Where was home again? I couldn't remember. This place was my home, wasn't it? This feeling was natural—this feeling was everything I needed. I was sure of that. Wasn't I?

I heard someone chuckling next to me. Who was that? Did I know them? Did it matter? I felt someone adjust me, and suddenly I could move my arms. What was that about? I stared at my hands as I held them above me. Why did I feel like now I could move them, that I needed to do something? I took a deep breath and tried to remember. Who was I? What was my purpose? Why was everything a blur?

A man stood above me as he stared at me. He appeared like a person looking down at a pathetic dog. I didn't like how he was looking at me—as if there was an internal instinct to punch him for giving me that look. What was this? Why did I feel so much hate when I felt so good?

I clenched my fist as I tried to get up. The man didn't move to stop me but kept watching, as if curious. I took a swing at him but quickly collapsed back down. The man laughed.

"Well, that is curious. I haven't had someone be so mad that the drug didn't work completely. Interesting. You must have a lot of hate deep down. I want to know your past even more."

My past? What was my past? Everything was such a haze, and something in me wanted to keep it that way. I wanted to forget my home and where I grew up. Had it really been that horrible? How did I end up here then?

An image came to the front of my mind. It was of a beautiful girl with gorgeous, dark hair and eyes. She was perfect for me, always smiling and telling me that she loved me.

"Chrys," I whispered. That was right—I was here looking for her. I needed to stop her. I needed to help her.

I stood up again and tried to get to the door. Everything was spinning, and I kept collapsing and getting back up. The man in the room watched me with intrigue.

"Do you really think you can leave that easily?" he asked. "Do you think I would let you walk out of here like this?"

I didn't know because I couldn't remember who he was or how I had ended up there. All I knew was I needed to find Chrys.

The man grabbed me and pulled me back. "I guess you need just a little bit more."

I shook my head and flailed, trying to get out of his hold, but he was much stronger than I was.

"No! I need to get out of here! I need to find her!"

Suddenly the door flung open and four figures stepped inside. They appeared blurry, and I had no idea who they could be.

"Get away from him!" I heard a woman demand. Her voice seemed familiar, but I couldn't place it. I glanced over the man's shoulder and found her to have red hair, but that was all I could make out.

"What, do you four think you can stop me?"

"Oh, we can. I can snap you out of your high with a wave of my hand. So let the human go."

The man got off me, and moments later I felt someone grab me and toss me over their shoulder.

"Don't worry, Huntley, we got you," the person holding me said.

I wasn't sure I could trust them, as I didn't know who they were, but I figured it was fine since they were saving me from this place.

"I'll get him back!" The man who had recently held me down yelled after us. "And he will never wake up from his dream!"

I didn't like how he said that, and I made a note not to go near him again whoever he was. Now I just needed to figure out who these people were and if they were going to help me find Chrys.

CHAPTER NINETEEN

Chrys

I circled around the mansion when finally I found a window that was open. I felt a little like Huntley as he snuck around the castle and got into Father's stuff all the time. Sometimes I went along with him and went into parts that I wasn't supposed to go into. Now I had access to the entire castle, and we didn't have to sneak around any longer.

The window was up high, but there was a tree that had some branches I could climb and reach it. I had no idea what kind of tree it was, as there weren't many in the underworld. I had heard that Hekate was a witch, so if she was like Maka, then she had a lot of plants growing in her garden. I had seen quite a few, but I didn't know anything about them. Perhaps someday Maka could teach me.

I climbed up the tree and was able to reach the window. I glanced inside to make sure that there was no one waiting for me. Lucky for me, there wasn't. I stepped inside and found it to be sort of Victorian-esque, which was not what I was expecting. Since she was a witch, I thought perhaps it would be more like Maka's house, but that was not the case. That was no matter, as all I needed were torches. I wasn't here to sightsee.

As I went through the room, which appeared to be a study with some couches, books, and a desk in the middle, I noticed that there was a lot of dust everywhere. Perhaps no one was home—which would be great for me. But I would keep an eye out, just in case.

I stuck my head out into the hallway and didn't see anyone. Even the floor was covered in dust. From what I could see, there were no footprints anywhere around here. I didn't know what to make of it but kept on listening for any noise. Perhaps she just didn't come up to the highest floor.

As I made my way through the upstairs, I checked every room. I had no idea where those torches could be, so I had to check thoroughly. I wasn't sure if they would be lit either, but I had a feeling the odds were they were. Why else would they be so magical to contain the ability to open the gates of Tartarus?

I had found a few bedrooms, another study, a large library, but nothing else. Why were there so many rooms? If it was only Maka here, it made no sense.

I ventured down to the second floor, careful not to touch the railing because it was disgustingly dusty and was making my skin itch. I stared up at the large glass ceiling that was above the stairwell to find it covered in cobwebs and spiders. It was so cool. I wish I could have brought Huntley with me as he would have had a lot of fun, looking at this place as well. Perhaps later, if

Hekate wasn't, in fact, here. I had a feeling once she figured out what I had done, I wouldn't be allowed back.

The second floor was much the same as the third. I still wasn't sure why one person would need so many rooms. Did she used to have a large family? Did she used to throw a lot of parties? From what I could tell, no one had been around here for quite some time. I hadn't heard about her moving or anything, and Charon would know of any rumors. He'd brought me here, which meant that she was here.

So where the heck was she? And why was this place like this? The more I peered around the second floor, the more I began to worry something either happened or this was some kind of trap. I took a deep breath. Perhaps it would have been smarter for me to simply knock on the front door, distract Hekate, and then search for it. Or since I was the queen of the underworld, I could ask to inspect the torches and then take them for myself. I was the queen after all.

Not that it mattered to her. If she cared about royalty, she wouldn't have screwed over my father like she did. So I didn't care if I was trespassing or if she might hate me. She probably already did.

I finished searching the last room that was part of the second floor. It had been a gaming room with old-style games such as billiards and darts. It was a little surprising, as I didn't think Hekate would be into that sort of stuff. Perhaps she really got into the 1800s. To each their own, I supposed.

I began to descend to the first floor. Light was shining through the top of the building now, highlighting the dust that was floating through the air. It took everything for me not to sneeze and just keep itching my skin. I hated the feeling of dust. It was the worst.

The first floor was open and didn't have many rooms. It was like that of a grand ballroom. I imagined dozens of people here, all in large dresses and suits, dancing around. Did that actually happen here? And if so, who came here? None of the gods were allowed into the underworld unless they were dead.

Unless the stories were true and Hekate had a secret passage that the gods could use to get to her.

What was with all these gods not doing as my father ordered? They always went behind his back to cause trouble and never allowed him anything he wanted. First his wife and then me. I felt my skin begin to get

warm. I just wanted all of them to disappear. My father
didn't deserve how he was treated by any of them. And
he didn't deserve to go to Tartarus.

There was still no sign of the torch. I had searched all
of the ballroom, the kitchen, and the few parlors that
were scattered downstairs, but there was nothing. I took
a deep breath, wondering where it could be and where
in the world Hekate was. I came upon my last door and
opened it.

The door creaked open, and I found a dark stairwell
that led down into a basement, I presumed. The walls
were rocky and cold, and I saw a flickering at the
bottom of the stairwell. Were those the torches? There
was only one way to find out.

I stepped slowly, as the stairs were cold and a little
wet. It was as if it were part of a cave. Was this the cave
that the gods could come through? I had so many
questions and not enough time to try to answer all of
them—all I knew was that I needed to find the torch.

There was no noise other than the echo of my steps
as I ventured down farther and farther. I wanted more
than anything to be quiet, but no matter how hard I
tried, the sound still echoed.

I made it down the stairs and found a large empty

room that simply had a cloth map hanging on one of the walls and two torches in front of the passage that led somewhere deeper into whatever cavern this was. Since there were two torches, I figured those were it. I took a deep breath and let it out slowly. This was it—I had found them.

Glancing over to the map, I had found that it was a map of the underworld, and then part of it showed a pathway that led to different realms. It seemed the tunnel where the torches stood branched off into different directions depending on where a god needed to go. Did all the gods use this? It seemed that it went to Olympus and deep into the ocean. Did Poseidon and Zeus come here as well? All under my father's nose?

I wondered if my father knew of this and that the underworld had been compromised all this time. Gods were not supposed to roam freely down here, and it seemed to me they had galas and parties all the time. And we weren't even invited. How could Hekate, a goddess of the underworld, do this? Why would she betray my father's trust?

Then again, she was the one who'd helped Demeter, so I should have figured where her loyalties lay. I took a deep breath and let it out slowly. After I got my father out of Tartarus, I would most definitely be dealing with her and all this backstabbing business.

Turning my attention back to the torches, I found that they wouldn't be hard to carry, but I wasn't sure how I was going to paddle the boat back to where Tartarus was. It was possible I could find somewhere to set them in the boat or hold them both with one hand. Either way, I would have to figure it out.

I reached out to grab them when I felt someone clutch my shoulder.

CHAPTER TWENTY

Huntley

Everything was beginning to make sense again, but I had one of the worst headaches I had ever had.

I was inside a flat in the middle of Hong Kong with Hermes, Maka, Mel, and Pothos. I had no idea how Mel and Pothos ended up joining the group, but I was thankful that they did as I knew there was safety in numbers when it came to dealing with Aether. That was what I had learned anyway.

Everything was still a bit hazy, but that asshole had kidnapped me and drugged me because he thought it was fun and to stop me from going after Chrys. I had proved him wrong, however, as I was able to focus on Chrys and try to leave. I was unsuccessful, of course, but I was still able to try. Then these four saved me.

Pothos handed me some sort of liquid. "Drink all of this."

"What is it?" I asked as I lifted it up. I was still shaking from the drug. So I did still have side effects even though I wasn't alive. Great.

"It's an herbal concoction," Maka explained. "It will help get rid of the rest of the drug and make it so the side effects wear off."

I took a sip and almost spat it out. "This is disgusting!"

"Stop your whining and drink it. Medicine isn't supposed to taste good—it's supposed to help you. Now drink it."

She had a point there. I drank it and tried not to gag.

It was so bad. But she was right. I needed it, so I had to keep drinking.

Hermes took a seat across from me at the table. "So, tell us what happened."

I glanced down at my cup, not sure where to start. "I... I went for a walk, like I do. Someone grabbed me and put a cloth over my head and bound me. Next thing I knew, I was in front of Aether. He did the whole bad guy rant on how I wanted the drug and that I should be happy I could take as much as I wanted without dying and without side effects, which apparently was somewhat a lie. It's not as bad as it used to be, but I definitely feel gross." I took a sip of the concoction. "Then I asked about Chrys. I made him tell me in exchange for telling me what Chrys asked him. He agreed."

I paused, not sure if I wanted to reveal the next information. I felt as if I were betraying Chrys. She was just trying to save her father, and yet here I was telling everyone what she was up to. But these were our friends—they wanted to help and had saved me. And they helped me save Chrys. They were the good guys.

"Chrys... is trying to open the gates to Tartarus. Apparently that paper gave the directions on what to do.

I'm not sure what it is, but she's on a mission."

Everyone glanced at each other. Maka took a deep breath. "This is a disaster. She can't do that or else all evil will be released on Earth."

I nodded. "Yeah, that's what Aether said. I asked him why he would help her do such a thing, but he simply said it was because he wanted the humans to fear you all once more. Typical bad guy stuff."

"He is a disgusting god," Mel spat out. "I may bring on nightmares for people, but he makes them live their nightmares. Most of those humans don't stand a chance getting out of there once they get in, and this isn't his only den. He has many throughout the world. He just prefers to stay at this one momentarily. He also drags gods down as well, making them stay with him for decades, if not more, with that drug. He needs to be brought down."

Maka nodded. "I agree, but first thing's first—we need to stop Chrys and knock some sense into her before it is too late. Not only will all the evil souls be let out, but so will Kronos. He will destroy everything like he sought to do all those years ago."

Kronos, from what I could remember, was afraid to die, and so he ate all his children except for Zeus. Zeus was somehow able to stop him, and they created Tartarus just for him. I gulped at the thought of the darkness I felt down there. Would all of that really be released? Would Chrys risk it all just for her father? Who was I kidding? Of course she would. And I didn't blame her.

"She is probably betting she can use her power to put everything back, but there is so much—and things that are a lot stronger than her. Kronos won't be going down even if she has the power over life and death—at least I don't think she will be able to take him out, on top of everything else." Hermes sighed. "We need to get to her, and fast. Do you have any idea where she could have gone?"

I shook my head. "No, he just said she was trying, but at least he knew the way to open it himself if need be."

"Great." Pothos rubbed his temples. "So we will have to worry about him after we stop Chrys."

"It would have to be something hard," Mel commented. "Otherwise Aether would have gone straight there. He has wanted to get his children back for quite some time."

Maka bit her lip. "I might know what she needs to

do, but I'm not sure."

We all stared at her. Hermes was the first to comment. "Well, spit it out."

"It… There have been rumors going around for some time. It's not as if anyone in the underworld has ever wanted to open the doors to Tartarus, so we never looked further into it—and information from the underworld never leaves. But I'm not sure if I should reveal it." Maka glanced around. Although I knew everyone here, she might not have known them as well as I did, being in the underworld for so long. Hermes used to trick Hades all the time and bug him, and I have no idea what she knew of the other two.

"Everyone at this table tried to help Chrys, even Hermes when he could. I trust them all with my life. You can tell them the truth," I said.

Maka nodded. "Right. Well, you all know the story of when Persephone wed Hades, correct? Hekate was the one who helped Demeter find her daughter, and because of that, Persephone could only stay in the underworld for a short amount of time."

That was the first time I was hearing about it. That was pretty messed up. I felt bad for Persephone, at least a little bit. I had a feeling, however, that the rest of them had heard the story.

"Well," she went on. "The way Hekate is able to navigate the underworld is through the torches she has. I'm sure the rest of you know those two torches if you have ever been to any of her galas."

The three of them glanced at each other. I raised an eyebrow. "What galas?"

Maka sighed. "Hekate has a way to let people travel from her home to other realms even though she is in the underworld. No one can step outside her home, however, but it is still a bit of a problem when you think about it. Anyway, the gate that is open at her home is open because of those torches. If one were to take those, they could potentially unlock the gate to Tartarus if they wanted."

That made partial sense. So they could light the way and therefore open a door.

"So she needs to take the torches. Is that very hard?"

All the gods laughed, as if what I said was a joke. I glared at them. "Well, answer me."

Maka patted my leg. "Huntley, she is the most feared goddess in all the realms. No one crosses her for a reason. She is strong, and she is scary. Even Zeus didn't deal with her because he was afraid of her."

So where was she when we were fighting Zeus? I sighed. "So Chrys is in danger?"

"Yeah, pretty much that is what we are saying." Pothos scratched his head. "But Chrys is honestly a lot stronger than Hekate probably is. I think. Yeah. Maybe."

I didn't like where this was going. "So should we go to Hekate's, or should we wait until after?"

Everyone was silent. It didn't seem anyone wanted to cross Hekate. I rubbed my face with my palm. I was already feeling better with the drink Maka had made me.

"What is she even thinking?" I whispered. "All this just to get Hades back? I mean, I liked him, but this is a little much, right? She is risking everything."

"And Hades risked everything for her," Maka explained. "She doesn't want to face the fact that a choice she made—although it would have happened eventually—caused the destruction of her father. No one blames Chrys for what happened, as it really was all Zeus's fault, but she probably doesn't see it that way."

Pothos added, "I'm surprised she was able to leave Aether's den. Most gods who fucked up and felt any guilt don't exactly leave there very easily. She has a strong will, as I presume Aether made her try the opium he has."

I nodded as I looked down at my cup. "Yeah, he did. He said she was interesting as she was able to snap out of it. She's strong, I give her that."

"And so are you." Pothos smiled. "I know how hard it was for you and when we got there, you were fighting back. That took courage and will."

"I'm just glad I was already dead. It didn't quite affect me like it did when I was alive. But that isn't what we are talking about. What should we do next?"

Hermes stood up. "I say we wait for her in front of Tartarus and stop her before it is too late. Who's with me?"

CHAPTER TWENTY-ONE

Chrys

I turned to find a woman who appeared to be almost the same age as me, staring at me with wide, creepy eyes. She wore a long black dress that made it look as if she had murdered her husband and now was lying to the police as she strode about her mansion. I gulped and gave her a smile.

"Hello there, you must be Hekate. I am Chrys, the queen of the underworld. I came down here to meet you since I am now the ruler over all this place."

She stared at me a moment longer, still not blinking. Maybe she didn't have parties—maybe she just had a mansion to be creepy.

"What are you doing here?"

"Um, I just said, I wanted to meet you."

She shook her head. "Then why did you climb my tree and go through the open window?"

Well, she had me there. "I knocked and no one answered. I got worried, so I decided to sneak in. I'm glad to see you are safe and sound."

"That's a lie. You never knocked. I would have heard. You snuck in, which made my spell trigger and everything was covered in dust so I could find you."

That was so cool. I wanted to know how she did that. But that wasn't the focus of today. "Wow, you must be one powerful witch for such a spell. Well, we must have had a misunderstanding because I most definitely knocked. Well, I'm glad to see you are well. I better be on my way."

"What are you searching for?" She ignored my request to try to leave.

"I wasn't searching for anything but you. This was the last room you could be in, so I came down here."

She turned her head the other way. "You aren't telling the truth. You are worse than your father."

I glared at her. "How dare you speak of the ruler of the underworld like that. He was a benevolent god who didn't deserve what happened to him."

"No, Zeus and Poseidon didn't deserve you killing them. They are suffering because of you."

I clenched my fist. "You were not there—they were trying to kill me!"

"You weren't supposed to be born, and Hades knew that. He broke his promise, and he got what was coming for him."

I bitch-slapped Hekate. Just straight up smacked her right across the cheek. I glared at her as she rubbed her cheek. "You take that back."

She was on me within seconds. I didn't know what I was expecting, but this wasn't it. Hekate had a strange atmosphere about her. She seemed old in the way she dressed and carried herself, and yet at the same time had a young appearance and was strong. I kicked her off me.

"What are you doing here, Chrysanthemum? What sort of monster did your father create?"

At that point, I decided not to hold back any longer. She didn't deserve it. I let the darkness roll off me in waves. At first she seemed shocked, but she didn't falter.

"I am taking these torches, and I am leaving this wretched place! I am sick of all you gods and how you have treated my father! I hope you all rot in Tartarus!"

Darkness spread out of me like hundreds of small lightning bolts. They clashed all around, darkening pieces of rock and charring the map that held the secret of these caves. I expected Hekate to be covered in marks, but she was unharmed. My eyes widened.

"How…?"

"Do you think you are the only goddess of darkness? Think again."

She was on me in a matter of seconds. I knew what darkness felt like as I was connected to the underworld, but I had never had it directly targeted at me. It felt as if everything that gave heat and light was sucked out of me in a matter of seconds. I gasped, trying to shake it off—trying to fix it with my mother's powers.

And luckily, I was able to.

But that didn't mean I would be able to take Hekate down. If she could control powers similar to mine, why was she alive? Why was she allowed to be here when I was ordered to die? It wasn't fair. I should have been able to live my life in the underworld without interference.

I summoned all the power I had—all the power I used to kill Zeus with. I directed it straight at her, but she was able to deflect it.

"How? How are you able to do that?!" I exclaimed. "If you could do that, why didn't you come help me when Zeus was trying to kill me?"

"Because I was rooting for Zeus! I didn't believe you would actually be able to stop him." She dabbed her eyes as if she had been crying all this time. "I loved him so much, and you destroyed him."

I had used a lot of power when I fought Zeus. I hated him with every fiber of my being and called upon everything I had to defeat him. I had found, since battling him, I could, in fact, draw even more power.

And I unleashed it all right then and there.

I was sick of it all. I was sick of everything against me. I was sick of how these gods were selfish and used any means to get what they wanted. I was sick of gods like Aether who abused everyone around them—I was sick of gods like Hekate who never saw the negative in the gods who abused others. I wanted them all destroyed. I wanted them all gone from existence.

Darkness swallowed the entire room—everything but the torches. I felt as if I was touching it all, taking away whatever life the air, rocks, and ground had and completely obliterating it. If there were plants here, they would have turned into dust. I wanted all of it gone —I wanted every living thing completely destroyed.

I took a deep breath, trying to make sure not to let it go and completely take out a piece of the underworld. I didn't want more to suffer. I didn't want to do what I had done on Earth two years ago. I just wanted Hekate dead.

As I took exhaled, I let the darkness fade. The two lights began to flicker again, bringing light back into the cave-like basement.

Hekate appeared like a frail elderly lady as she lay on the ground where she once stood. My heart was racing —I was afraid that she would be fine after all that, as she was able to block my earlier attacks.

I went to grab the torches when something clutched

my leg. I glanced down to find it was Hekate. I screamed.

Her skin was slowly regenerating, as if she were drinking from the fountain of youth. Her white hair slowly turned back to the dark color it once was.

"How dare you attack me in cold blood like that!"

"Just die!" I screamed as I kicked her in the side. She didn't let go of my foot.

"Zeus himself was afraid of me! Your father feared me! I am the most powerful goddess!"

She dug her nails into my skin. I let out a scream as I kicked her again. I glanced around. I could almost reach the torches.

The torches which happened to be on large stakes.

I reached forward and was able to grab the stake. I pulled the torch out and held on to the handle. Quickly I spun around and stabbed Hekate straight in the torso, pinning her down to the ground.

She screamed as she let go of my leg. I jumped back and watched her try to unpin herself. She wasn't able to get enough strength to pull it out.

As fast as I could, I grabbed the other torch and went straight for the gondola that Charon had left for me. I climbed up the stairs to find that the entire place was no longer covered in dust but nicely clean and full of light and power.

"What the—" I shook my head. I didn't have time for this. I needed to get out of there.

"I'll get you, Chrys! If it is the last thing I do!" I heard Hekate scream.

That was my cue. I headed to the front door and ran straight for my gondola when I felt something tackle me to the ground. I dropped both the torches. Hekate turned me around and began clawing at my skin.

"What the fuck is wrong with you?" I exclaimed.

"I'll do everything I can to stop you from opening those gates! What has died and was sent there should never be released! I am the protector of Tartarus, and I'll do whatever it takes."

Well, I couldn't blame her. I glanced around for something to use as a weapon as it seemed that neither of us could take the other out with our powers. I saw one of the torches and grabbed it.

I set Hekate's hair on fire. It went up quickly, the once dark strands now one big flame. She screamed bloody murder as she tried to bat it out. Her hands began to burn and become black. I almost vomited from the stench of burned hair and flesh. As she flailed around and searched for something to put it out, I grabbed the other torch and made it to the gondola.

Hekate followed but only to dunk her hair into the water. I wondered what effects the River Mnemosyne would do to her since it wasn't her memories, but at that point I definitely didn't care. I held on to the torches with one hand and paddled away as fast as I could toward the complete opposite side of the underworld.

CHAPTER TWENTY-TWO

Huntley

Hermes couldn't fly everyone down to the underworld, so he took me and Pothos, while Mel rode with Maka in her motorboat. The three of them headed straight for Tartarus, but Hermes and I decided to head toward

Hekate's place just to make sure Hekate didn't do anything to Chrys. For the way Hermes entered, it was on the way. I had no idea still how Hermes got into the underworld, so I figured he was telling the truth there.

As always, I had to have a blindfold on as we entered. At that point, Hermes should know that Chrys didn't care if he came into the underworld, but I supposed it was just habit. And in case something happened. Gods lived for a long time, so it was always possible that something would go wrong.

It was strange going from the mortal realm to the underworld. It was like going through almost something jellylike, but once you were completely inside, it no longer felt like that. I wondered if that was what going through the stargate was like in *Stargate SG-1*. I had watched a few episodes when I was little and always wished that I could travel to another planet and away from my parents. Little did I know that there were different worlds, and they had to do with Greek mythology, not Atlantis and other aliens.

Then again, maybe the other mythologies were true and they had different realms. Wouldn't that be interesting?

Once we were completely inside and had traveled

quite a ways, Hermes took the blindfold off me. He was carrying me like a princess. While it felt odd, I had to admit it was a lot more comfortable than being on his back.

"It's not far from here to Hekate's. Hopefully, Chrys hasn't been there or is just showing up so we don't even have to deal with Hekate," Hermes said.

"Is she really that terrifying to deal with? I mean, Chrys is pretty strong. I doubt she will have any problems."

"Well, normally I would agree, but Hekate is a sorceress who deals with dark magic. She can manipulate darkness, and it doesn't affect her like it does everyone else."

"Meaning if Chrys uses her powers, Hekate won't be affected."

"Exactly, so it will just turn into a fistfight more than likely. And Hekate doesn't play fair when it comes to fistfights."

I sighed. "Seriously? Why does everything have to be complicated with you gods?"

"Well, do you want her to open Tartarus? It's a good thing Hekate is as powerful as she is. Otherwise, someone could have done something a long time ago."

"That's fair, I guess."

"The other problem, however, is that Hekate was pretty close to Zeus. She has been in mourning since his death. She probably blames Chrys for all that, so she will be extra angry when she fights. And depending on how Chrys approaches her... Let's just say Hekate doesn't like it when people trespass."

Oh, that was just great. I knew better than to piss off a goddess at that point, but Chrys wasn't as fragile as I was. She also didn't know what Hekate was capable of. She probably figured if she could take down Zeus, then she had nothing to fear. Hermes seemed to disagree with that. I just prayed that she was all right or hadn't quite arrived at Hekate's, and we could stop this before it all started.

But if I had learned anything from all my years with these gods, nothing ever went according to plan.

"What if we are wrong though? What if Chrys isn't doing all this, but Aether just wanted to cause problems for us?"

"Chrys has been acting strange though. I don't think, in this instance, that Aether is lying to us."

I frowned. "But if he was, what if Chrys won't forgive me for thinking she was up to no good? Or even if she is doing this, do you think she will be mad that I went and followed her behind her back?"

Hermes shook his head. "Even if she is mad, we need to stop this. No good will come from opening those gates. Everything will be released—everything the gods had to fight with all their might to put away. And that was at different times. I don't know if we would be able to defeat it all if it attacked at once. We might all be doomed. So a martial fight would be nothing compared to if she succeeds."

That made sense. For the greater good and all that. I still had my doubts she would do such a thing, but there was also the possibility that she thought she could grab her father and then quickly get out of there. I took a deep breath and sighed.

"Why do you think she is willing to risk it all?"

"Because she feels responsible, and mourning can cause you not to think straight. Death is a horrible thing, and on top of that, she knows where her father is and what is happening to him. She just couldn't live with it and figured she would deal with the consequences later. Or she doesn't truly understand the consequences."

That made sense. If Chrys had died, I probably would

have tried everything I could to get her back, even as a human. I could understand her pain a little.

We approached a large mansion that appeared like something on the outskirts of London. If I didn't know better, Hekate was just some Victorian aristocrat who had way too much money and time on her hands. These gods were always so peculiar in what they liked about human culture, and they stuck to that.

As we got closer, we noticed smoke and someone lying on the ground next to the entrance.

"What in the world...?" Hermes murmured as he went to land next to the figure.

I almost vomited as a vile odor overcame my senses. It smelled of burned hair and skin—something no human should ever have to inhale. The body that lay on the ground was bald with burn marks all over her scalp and hands. I looked away as Hermes bent next to her.

"Hekate! What happened?" Hermes asked, as if we didn't know. I mean, we didn't know the exact details, but we knew it had something to do with Chrys.

"That horrible woman came and took the torches! She set me on fire, and now she is heading toward Tartarus!" the woman yelled. I was surprised she was still alive, but as I glanced back at her, it was apparent that she was healing slowly. Some of the wounds I had seen were already closed up.

I couldn't believe Chrys would set someone on fire like that, but then again I wasn't sure what exactly had happened. If her power of darkness had no effect on Hekate, then she would have had to do something to stop her. But still, that was not something I wanted to ever experience.

Hermes turned to me. "We have to hurry and go stop her!"

CHAPTER TWENTY-THREE

Chrys

I rowed as fast as I could. Hekate could heal and do all sorts of things I didn't know were possible—for all I knew, she could easily fly after me and tear me to shreds.

I felt bad for setting her hair on fire like that, but it was the only thing I could do in the situation. She was going to rip me into a million pieces if I didn't try to stop her. What else could I have done?

I tried to slow my breathing down to calm myself, but it was no use. I was heading to Tartarus where I could potentially destroy everything. I still wasn't sure if it was the right decision, but I couldn't go on living like this. I wanted my father back, and I wasn't afraid of doing what it took. Between the two of us, we would be able to put everything back to how it was and he would be where he belongs. We didn't have to worry— just because Tartarus was open didn't mean that everything would escape the underworld—it just meant it was free from the agonizing hell that was that deep, dark place.

Even in my small amount of time down there, it was horrible. I couldn't imagine what my father was going through. Was he just falling in complete darkness— hearing the voices of all the souls he had sent into Tartarus? Or was Kronos there, torturing him for tying him down into that hellish landscape? The more I thought about it, the more my heart hurt. My father didn't deserve such an eternity. I had to do something.

Anyone else in my shoes would do the same. I had no doubt in my mind. There were tales of heroes coming to save their loved ones all the time. How was this any different? If the idea of opening Tartarus should never be thought, then why did those torches exist? I was fulfilling their purpose. This needed to be done.

At least that was what I kept telling myself.

I turned onto the River Styx and kept rowing, careful not to end up in the water again. This would lead me to Tartarus. I could see the castle in the distance. Soon it would be my father's castle once again, and I wouldn't have to rule. He would have his spot where he belonged.

I didn't see Charon anywhere, which was a good thing as he would try to lead me back to the castle. If I didn't go with him that way, he would start to question what I was doing and more than likely try to stop me. I couldn't let that happen.

The closer I rowed toward Tartarus, the slower the stream was. It was as if even the stream didn't want to go near the place. I used the paddle to go a bit faster, still glancing behind my back for anyone. So far, there was no one.

I expected someone to come stop me even if Hekate

was the only one who knew what I was up to. I was thankful no one could transport in an instant here like they could on Earth. Although if that were the case, then I could have been to Tartarus already.

Even though I could see Tartarus from the castle, it was much different rowing up to it. The waterfall of souls seemed larger as they went down into the pit of darkness. The River Styx pooled right in front of the entrance, and I would be able to get out and put the torches at the door. I had seen the door once when I was much younger. I had been running around, adventuring as one did, and came upon it. Father found me and scolded me to never go near that place again.

Look at me now, Father.

I just prayed that I would be able to put everything back. The fear ate at my brain, but I couldn't spend time worrying about that when I needed to save him.

As I stopped my boat, I heard my name being called. I turned to find Maka in a motorboat heading in my direction. It was moving fast, and I wondered how long she had that. With her were two figures. I squinted to realize they were Pothos and Mel.

I wanted to ask how and why in the world they were down here, but I knew at this point I had no time to waste. I moved the boat toward the shore and jumped off, running toward the gate.

"Don't do it, Chrys! You can't! You will destroy everything! Don't you realize that?" Maka yelled.

I shook my head. "I don't care! I need him back! He doesn't deserve this!"

"And we agree with you! I don't want him in there either, but this is not the way!"

Shaking my head, I put one of the torches in the slot on one side of the door. "Then what is? No one is going to help me get him back! There is no other way! I have gone through every book and every paper. This is the only way!"

They arrived to the shore and were running toward me.

Maka reached out for me. "Chrys, please. Listen to me."

Tears were running down my face. "It hurts. Every day, no matter what I do. It is my fault he is dead, and I can't live like this. I can fix whatever happens, but first I need him back."

Mel stepped toward me slowly. "We will help you get him back, but first let's discuss what will really happen when you open this door."

"Mel is right," Pothos interjected. "I don't think you quite realize what you are doing."

"I do, you guys. I really do know what I am doing. And you can't stop me."

CHAPTER TWENTY-FOUR

Huntley

Hermes was moving as fast as he could toward Tartarus. I never knew he could fly so quickly. It was sort of making me sick, as it was like a roller coaster, but Hermes would move each and every way, as if he was looking for the correct current.

I wanted to tell him to slow down just a tad, as I feared he would drop me and I would go plummeting down, but I knew that would be a stupid request. So I held on tightly and prayed that everything would wind up all right.

Chrys was making a big mistake, although it was one I could understand. I just wished that she had come to me—or had gone to any of us—and talked about how she was feeling. She kept it bottled inside, which probably ate at her even more.

She knew what she was doing was wrong, and she believed it was the only way to save her father. Because of this, she stayed quiet until she found the information she wanted.

I wanted to hug her. I wanted to tell her it was all right and that we would all figure out a way to get her father back, but I wasn't sure that would be possible. For all I knew, which wasn't much, this was indeed the only way to save him. And no one would agree to it, which was why she'd acted on her own.

If I had known the truth, would I have tried to help her? Or would I have simply sided with the other gods and agreed it was too dangerous? By the sounds of it, there were a lot of horrible things down there. What if they were able to get out of the underworld and make their way to Earth? They could destroy everything.

I still wasn't sure why Aether wanted to help Chrys or what he had to gain. I understood how he believed the gods were forgotten, as they were taught like some fictional tale in history classes, but would destroying the world really make that any better? I didn't think it would, but I supposed I was just some kid who didn't know anything.

After thousands of years, I believed these gods started to lose their minds. It was the only explanation.

"Are we there yet?" I asked Hermes, trying to calm myself down. There was so much at stake now I wasn't even sure my mind could comprehend it.

"See that big waterfall of souls before us?"

I nodded. "Yup."

"That is where we are going, so no. Not quite there."

"Right."

Tartarus, although a horrible, horrible place, was quite beautiful to look at. It was like a huge hole in the sky where bluish souls rained down, making one of the most wonderful sceneries that I had ever seen. It was bigger than what I believed Niagara Falls was, at least from the pictures I had seen. I just tried not to think about where the souls were going.

During my time in Tartarus, I never imagined I could be saved. I supposed I really was just in this part of the waterfall before I was truly in the darkness that went through to the center of the world. I couldn't imagine what it was like down there and what all those souls were experiencing. Was it like fire? Was it just dark? Could you see any other soul? Were Hades, Poseidon, and Zeus just annoying each other for all eternity? I had no idea, and I doubted anyone else really knew.

As we approached, I could see Maka's boat. She was able to reach Chrys before she opened the gate, thank goodness. If they were able to hold her off until we got there, I was sure I could calm her down and get her to come back with us.

Hermes landed behind Pothos and Mel. Chrys's eyes widened as she saw me.

"Were you the one who figured out what I was doing?" Her eyes were already full of tears as she held the second torch. "Did you follow me?"

"I... All of us were concerned. You weren't acting normal," I began. "I just wanted to make sure you were safe."

She frowned as if conflicted. She glanced around at everyone. I wondered if it made her feel supported or if she was beginning to feel like the entire world was against her. She took a deep breath.

"I just want him back. I don't care what it takes."

I shook my head. "No, Chrys, you don't know if this will bring him back or if it will just cause more problems. Please, just hear us out."

"I have done things I can't go back on. If I found out this is the only way to get my father back, I doubt I'll have a second chance in retrieving those torches." She turned to the gate. "So there is no turning back at this point."

We all dove toward her to stop her, but it was too late. The torch went into the slot, and the gate of Tartarus was now open.

And I, well, I expected a little more.

The door slowly opened, and there wasn't anything. Nothing was coming out of it; there was no sound. Nothing. Everyone glanced around as if trying to figure out what exactly had happened.

Chrys peered around and slowly stepped inside. I tried to grab her wrist, but it was too late. The moment she went inside, a big roar sounded and darkness came pouring out of the gate.

CHAPTER TWENTY-FIVE

Chrys

I was surrounded by darkness. I couldn't hear anything or see far in front of me. I wanted to call out, but I felt as if something was stopping me.

Moving forward, I knew I couldn't turn back. It was

as if something had blocked my way out. Did the gate actually not let anyone out but only let people in? If that were the case, then perhaps now I was dead and there would be no leaving Tartarus now.

Well, at least I got what I deserved.

I glanced all around, searching for someone—anyone —but all I saw was darkness. I kept on moving, praying that there would be something that would answer my questions.

This should have worked. There was no reason for my father not to write that note if it wasn't true. Perhaps Aether had been lying to me. I highly doubted it, however, as he seemed to want the gate to be open and had no reason to send me to Tartarus that I could tell.

So was I really considered dead, or was this some strange test to see if I really was worthy to open the gates or something? I had a feeling it was the latter. As I kept moving forward, I saw a small light. I hurried to it to find my father.

I knelt down beside him and wrapped my arms around him. "Thank goodness it's you. Father, I'm so happy."

He wore the same suit he had on when he was killed by Zeus. As he looked up at me, his eyes was filled with anger and rage.

"What have you done?"

Thank you so much for reading! Readers like you make it possible for authors like me to write stories! If you could spare a moment and leave a review on Amazon, Goodreads, BookBub, and wherever you like to buy books, that would mean the world to me! It really helps authors like me to succeed in the publishing world.

A big thank you again for your patronage. I hope you will check out my other work!

I want to thank everyone who made this novel possible. A big thank you to my editor Justin and Annie who hopefully hasn't gotten sick of reading my stories yet. Thank you to Biserka Design for the amazing covers for this series! I love them lot! A special thank you to Dr. Almira Poudrier at ASU for answering my questions about Greek Mythology as things get weird and confusing and even more weird. And, lastly, thank you to my husband and parents who are always supporting me.

Dani Hoots is a science fiction, fantasy, romance, and young adult author who loves anything with a story. She has a B.S. in Anthropology, a Masters of Urban and Environmental Planning, a Certificate in Novel Writing from Arizona State University, and a BS in Herbal Science from Bastyr University.

Currently she is working on a YA urban fantasy series called Daughter of Hades, a YA urban fantasy series called The Wonderland Chronicles, a historic fantasy vampire series called A World of Vampires, and a YA sci-fi series called Sanshlian Series.

She has also started up an indie publishing company called FoxTales Press. She also works with Anthill Studios in creating comics through Antik Comics.

Her hobbies include reading, watching anime, cooking, studying different languages, wire walking, hula hoop, and working with plants. She is also an herbalist and sells her concoctions on FoxCraft Apothecary. She lives in Phoenix with her husband and visits Seattle often.

Feel free to email her with any questions you might have!
danihootsauthor@gmail.com